D0456211

YEARLING BOOKS/YOUNG YEARLINGS/YEARLING CLASSICS are designed especially to entertain and enlighten young people. Patricia Reilly Giff, consultant to this series, received her bachelor's degree from Marymount College and a master's degree in history from St. John's University. She holds a Professional Diploma in Reading and a Doctorate of Humane Letters from Hofstra University. She was a teacher and reading consultant for many years, and is the author of numerous books for young readers.

For a complete listing of all Yearling titles, write to Dell Readers Service, P.O. Box 1045, South Holland, IL 60473.

Someday I'll Laugh About This

by Linda Crew

For Jennifer,
Hope you'll get
a laugh out of this now!
Linda Crew
1993

A Yearling Book

Published by
Dell Publishing
a division of
Bantam Doubleday Dell Publishing Group, Inc.
666 Fifth Avenue
New York, New York 10103

"Bobby's Girl" (Henry Hoffman & Gary Klein)
1962 American Metropolitan Ent. Inc. (all rights reserved)
"You Gotta Have Heart" Copyright © 1955, 1957 Frank Music
Copyright © renewed 1983 Richard Adler Music and
  J & J Ross Company
All rights administered by the Songwriters Guild of America

ISBN: 0-440-40679-X

Reprinted by arrangement with Delacorte Press

Printed in the United States of America

August 1992

10 9 8 7 6 5 4 3 2 1

OPM

For my parents,
Warren Welch
and
Marolyn Schumacher Welch.
Thanks for the memories.
And for Grampa Schu,
who started it all.

Someday
I'll Laugh
About This

Chapter One

"Come on, Shelby," my brother Danny says. "You already got the good bed. Gimme a turn with the binoculars."

"In a minute." I'm checking out these lover types down on the beach. It's all misty white now, the way it gets when the sun's close to setting and the light floods in at a slant, fuzzing off the edges of things. I'll bet they think they're all alone—this boy and girl—the way they take turns chasing each other and playing huggy-grabby when one gets caught. They don't realize anything happening on the beach is a show for the people in the cabins along here. And this loft window facing north has the best view of all. That's why we always fight for it.

"Shelby . . ." Danny flops on the bed next to me, creaking the springs.

"I said, just a minute."

They're down at the creek now. It's all of three inches deep where it fans out across the sand, but the guy makes a big deal of carrying the girl across. I can tell she's laughing, dangling her sandals from her toes. What's so funny? I follow them with the binoculars as they come up the beach, hands stuck in the back pockets of each other's jeans. I guide the circle of my vision to the left until they disappear behind the point. I jerk the binoculars up. Now the new house out there wobbles into view.

The house on the point. I used to be able to watch the sun dropping behind the horizon right there. Now I'm looking at this jumble of goofy roof planes . . . I yank the binoculars away.

"Hey, look!" Danny says. "They're here!"

Down on the lawn, a mini-van pulls in alongside our car.

I drop the binoculars on the quilt and elbow past him down the steep wooden stairs to meet our cousins. Our vacation with them at Sea Haven is always a big deal, but this year especially. I haven't seen Kirsten since last fall. That's when they moved away from our town, Corvallis, Oregon, because Uncle Don got a new hotshot job in computer software. Now they live up in Bellevue, Washington.

Jason's first out of the van. At least I think it's Jason. He sure isn't the curly-headed, buck-toothed little kid in cut-offs I remember. Now his blond hair is short. He's wearing red and orange jams and a T-shirt with a crazy dog riding a motorcycle on it. When he smiles, the sun glints off a mouthful of braces.

He punches Danny's arm. "Hey, dude."

For an instant Danny looks surprised at Jason's clothes. Then he says, "I tried to get dibs on the good bed, but Shelby hogged it first."

Someday I'll Laugh About This

"Well, it's our turn," I say. "Look where Kirsten wrote it in the log last year if you don't believe me."

Jason shrugs and puckers his chin up real ugly. "Who cares?"

Huh. I thought he'd be bugged. He always used to act like it mattered a lot.

Aunt Margo gets out, hugs Mom, and starts right in talking about how proud she is of herself for making this seven-hour drive on her own. She had to because Uncle Don can't come until our second week here. She's wearing this rose-colored jogging suit with a matching sweatband. Somehow she always manages to look like Mom's younger sister, even though she's older. Maybe it's because Mom's starting to get a little gray right where her hair parts in the middle. Aunt Margo's hair is still all dark, though. It's curly, too, and it looks kind of neat the way she's got it tucked up under the sweatband.

"Shelby Lynn Graham," Mom says. "You're soaked! I hope you weren't sitting on the sofa."

"I wasn't."

"Yeah," Danny says. "She was lying on the bed."

I give him a shove. Why does he always have to be such a tattletale?

Mom frowns. "I wish you kids would just put on your bathing suits if you're going to get wet."

I roll my eyes. She knows perfectly well that the first thing we have to do when we get to Sea Haven is run down on the beach. I'll bet in all the years our family's been coming to Gramma and Grampa B.'s cabin, nobody ever, *ever* stopped to put on their bathing suit before

3

Linda Crew

they headed down the stone steps. I'll bet *she* never did, back when she and Margo and Uncle Jack used to come with Gramma and Grampa B.

"How you doing, Shelb?" Margo says, hugging me. Then she backs up to get a good look. She fluffs out my long, frizzy hair. "Look at all this! Are you going for a record or what?" Her smile fades as over my shoulder she catches sight of the new house on the point. "Well," she says to Mom, "you weren't kidding, were you, Nancy?"

"I told you it was huge."

The house on the point, the house on the point. I'm sick of it. Maybe if they didn't talk about it so much it'd be easier to forget. Ever since we watched the builders break ground in the spring this is all I've heard. "Can they *do* that?" Mom's probably said a million times by now. "We always thought the state owned that plot, sticking out over the rocks the way it does." Then she usually starts in about the wild strawberries they bulldozed away.

"Mom and Dad doing okay?" Margo asks Mom. Gramma and Grampa still live in Corvallis, too, so even though I know Margo calls them a lot, Mom's always the one with the most up-to-date report.

"Oh sure, they're fine. I was hoping we'd get them to come for more than just the last weekend, but you know how Dad is about leaving his garden this time of year."

Margo nods and turns to Danny. "Now here's a kid who's not afraid of a haircut. I like it."

4

I run my hand up the back of his head. "Feels so weird. Like splinters."

Danny jerks away. "Better than a mophead like you've got."

"Can you believe it, Margo?" Mom says. "Our kids with crew cuts." Margo shakes her head. "Between that and the high-topped tennis shoes, I feel like I'm in a fifties time warp."

"Maybe it's true what they say," Mom says. "The more things change, the more they stay the same."

Daddy pulls two more suitcases from the back of Aunt Margo's van. "Next they'll be bugging *me* to get a crew cut. Wouldn't that be something, after hearing it from my folks all those years?"

"No we won't," I say. I like Daddy's bushy hair and beard. He and I can be bushy together.

Margo's looking at Danny. "I can never get over this kid's eyelashes, Nancy. And what a waste on a boy."

Danny squirms, his face bright pink under his freckles. Nothing he hates more in the whole world than people fussing over his big blue eyes and long black lashes.

"Aunt Nancy?" Five-year-old Brandon is out of the van and tugging at Mom's sweater sleeve. He's clutching this tattered toy catalog. "Now. Here's the next thing I'm going to get for my Transformer collection . . ."

"That's it, sweetie," Aunt Margo says wearily, patting him on the head and heading for the cabin. "You tell Aunt Nancy *all* about it."

Funny. Kirsten isn't getting out of the van. I go over to the open sliding door.

"Hi! Come on, I'll help you carry your stuff up."

Kirsten eases out of the middle seat and stretches. She looks different. Older. Her long dark hair's been chopped short and flipped over to one side. She's wearing these superclean white stirrup pants. And something else . . . I sniff. Perfume.

She yawns. "Hi, Shelby."

"Gee, you're really tan." Suddenly I feel grimy in my wet jeans and ragged sweatshirt.

She checks her bare arm like she's making sure the toasty color hasn't faded. Then she shivers. "Why does it always have to be so cold here?" She pulls a bulky purple sweater on over her tank top and crosses her arms.

"Don't you want to go in?"

She doesn't answer.

"Hey, what's the matter?"

She sighs. "I'm sorry. It's just that after seven straight hours of Jason punching me, and Brandon yapping about Transformers . . ." She trails off, looking down the beach. To our left, the sun's setting with a lot of pink cotton-candy clouds. It's gorgeous, but from the bleak look on Kirsten's face you'd think she was staring at a rainstorm over a garbage dump or something. "I mean, sure, it's great to see you," she goes on, "but really, were you all that thrilled about coming this year?"

"Well, gee . . ." I stuff my hands in my pockets. "I guess I *was* looking forward to it."

"Oh."

"Sort of," I add, somehow embarrassed.

"Well, it's nothing personal, Shelb. Not personal about

6

you, I mean. It's just that . . . when you have a boy-friend . . . having to leave for two whole weeks . . ."

I suck in my breath. "You have a boyfriend?" She's thirteen now, just one year older than me. Suddenly it seems like ten.

"Mmm-hm. Do you?"

"Uh, no." A month ago I might have stretched facts and called Jeremy Harrison a boyfriend, but after that disaster at Heather Gray's boy-girl birthday party . . . no way. And even though Dad says it means he likes me, I don't think Willy Stark shooting peas at me with a straw in the cafeteria really counts. On the other hand, what if Dad's right? I study Kirsten's face. "How do you know he's your boyfriend?"

Her black eyebrows go up. Then she laughs, holding out her hand. On one finger is a boy's silver ring, a wad of first-aid tape wrapped around it to keep it from slipping off.

"He *gave* that to you?" I'm not stupid. Even I know the difference between a ring on your finger and a pea in your eye.

Kirsten sighs. "Like Troy says, it's going to be *death* to be apart like this."

A funny ache grabs my chest. I can't imagine anyone feeling it would be death to be away from me, not now, not ever.

Kirsten takes a large, flowered cosmetic bag and a stack of magazines from the backseat and heads toward the cabin.

Lugging her suitcase, I trail behind.

In the kitchen, Mom's throwing out a dried-up vase of pearly everlasting Gramma B. left the weekend before.

"Well, look at *you*," she says to Kirsten. She and Aunt Margo trade these knowing looks. "Margo, she's you all over again."

Kirsten lowers her lavender eyelids and blushes as Mom and Margo gaze at her with mushy expressions.

So what's the big deal?

Aw, shoot. Anyone with eyes can *see* what the big deal is.

Kirsten's gone and grown up!

Chapter Two

"**A**re you coming or not?" Kirsten yells.

I look up. She's stopped at a rise in the bluff trail ahead of me, hands on her hips. *Impatience Against a Blue Sky* you could call this picture.

I wave a wait-a-minute signal. No use trying to shout about wanting to look at the shells. What doesn't get drowned by the boom of breakers on the rocks gets carried away on the wind.

I'm crouching beside a freshwater brook that spills over the big flat rocks into the ocean. Gramma B. says Indians used to camp here. They left the remains of their shellfish feasts here for so long, the ground is pure white. I wonder, did an Indian girl my age ever stand on this very spot?

"Shelby, *come on!*"

I drop a lavender-tinted chip into my pocket. Spreading my arms for balance, I cross the brook's flat stepping-stones and climb the path up through the crumbling sand cliffs. What's the big hurry? Getting to the post office quicker doesn't have anything to do with whether or not Kirsten will actually find a letter from Troy in the general-delivery mail.

Linda Crew

Dumb old Troy. I don't even know him and I hate him already. If it wasn't for Troy, Kirsten could be having fun. She'd have joined our pillow fight in the loft last night. Heck, she would have started it, swinging her pillow like the wild monkey she used to be instead of lying there sniffling into it.

"Hurry up, will you?"

"If you don't get off my case," I say, "I'm not going to walk into Perpetua with you again. And they won't let you go alone."

That shuts her up for a minute.

"And anyway," I go on, "isn't it a little soon to be looking for a letter? You just got here."

"He promised to mail something before I even left."

"You're kidding. Kirsten, do you realize how silly that is?"

She turns and sniffs. "Wait till *you* have a boyfriend. Then you won't think so."

A boyfriend? Me? She says this like she's assuming I will. As for me, I have serious doubts.

I hate boys. Especially Jeremy Harrison. I used to like him because he lived down the street and he always chose me for his baseball team. So when Heather Gray dreamed up her stupid girls-ask-boys birthday party, Mom says, "Oh, ask Jeremy. He's your friend, isn't he?" Bad advice. I wind up standing around with all the girls on the opposite side of Heather's rec room from the boys, hot and uncomfortable in this dopey dress and pinchy shoes. It doesn't help when Jeremy finally comes across and asks me to dance, only when I step forward

10

into no-man's-land it turns out he's talking to this girl named Jessica, who's standing a little behind me. And before the party's over—it seems a million years long—it gets back to me that Jeremy's telling everyone his mother made him come with me.

This is fun? This is what becoming a teenager's going to be like? One party and I've had enough.

"I don't want a boyfriend," I tell Kirsten.

"Well, you will."

Huh. I shuffle after her.

We make our way through the twisting maze of paths that used to be a road. Gramma B. told us that before Highway 101 was built, people traveled on the beach at low tide. Then, right where Sea Haven sits in the curve of the point, they drove their Model Ts up onto the bluffs.

Now the trail leads out of the bushes and cuts through the short grass. Ahead is the Pacific Breakers Motel.

I stop as we pass the smelt cove. "I wish you'd been here with us for the smelt run in June." I love it when everybody for miles around comes with hip boots and nets to scoop up the little fish as they crash in with the waves. We kids grab them bare-handed while they flip around our legs. Kirsten used to catch more than anybody.

But now she shrugs. "Smelt are slithery."

"Come on. That never bothered you before."

"So I've changed."

No kidding.

We walk past the motel and the newer summer houses and finally get to my favorite streets, the ones with all the

11

little old shingled cottages. They have real yards here, with blue hydrangeas and pink roses twining up the telephone poles.

But Kirsten doesn't look at any of this. You can tell she has just one thing on her mind as she cuts through the Ain't Mad at Nobody gas station and dashes across the highway to the squatty brick post office.

I trail up the cement steps behind her.

Funny thing—once we're inside the stuffy little building, she starts acting like picking up the mail is just something she happened to think of as she was walking by. She rests one elbow on the counter in front of the window.

"Any mail for the Stewart family, general delivery?"

"Or the Grahams?" I put in.

The woman eyes us. "Mebbe," she says. Her hair is this wimpy knot at the back of her head, and she wears the same old button-up sweater as always. I guess it was blue once, but that was a long time ago.

She pulls a handful of letters from a pigeonhole and thumbs through them as slowly as possible. She always likes to make us wait. Finally she stops at a fat white envelope.

Kirsten reaches for it.

The woman holds it away. "You Shelby Graham?"

Kirsten's face goes pink. She backs up a step.

"Uh, that's me," I say. I don't dare look at Kirsten. She'd probably like to smack me.

The postmistress frowns at the envelope and sets it on

her scale. She frowns even harder when there's no postage due. Finally she lays it on the counter.

I snatch it up before she can change her mind. It's from Jane! Jane's been my best friend since second grade, only now she got dragged off to a place called Salina, Kansas, after her parents' divorce. Good old Jane! I guess she made a note of the dates I said we'd be here.

"Oh, no! Check it out!" A long letter written on yellow toilet paper. I glance over my shoulder. The postmistress is still watching us, so I gather up the tissue. "Come on, let's go." Outside, I sit down on the cement steps and start reading.

"That lady makes me so mad," Kirsten mutters.

"Oh, you know she's always like that. You wouldn't care if you'd gotten a letter." I start reading about Jane trying to baby-sit a family of five kids. "Wow, listen to this—"

"Spare me," Kirsten snaps.

"Come on, you don't have to get grouchy just because I got mail and you didn't."

Kirsten sniffs. "Mail from a girl."

"Hey, wait a minute. Since when is a letter from a girl not as good as *no* mail from a boy?"

"Okay, so you got a letter and I didn't. Do you have to read it now? I've got stuff to buy."

I let out a big sigh, roll up the letter, and stuff it in my jeans pocket. "If it was from Troy, you'd expect me to wait for you." I kick at the gravel. "Anyway, first we have to stop at Tillie's. I promised Brandon the boats."

Banana boats—a banana split in a plastic boat—are

13

the specialty at Tillie the Whale's Ice Cream. We get ours and eat them as we stroll down the town's one stretch of sidewalk.

No fancy shops with soaps and flowery stuff, no fake storefronts to make the place look like a Western town or a Swiss village. The stores are funky, one of a kind, selling funny combinations of things—quilts and driftwood, dolls and agates, books and kites. Everything seems pretty much the same as always, except for the grocery store's new sign out front advertising a tanning booth.

Kirsten peers in the window of a little gift shop. "Look at these cute barrettes, Shelby. Those would look really neat on you. Let's go in and see how much they are."

"Nah," I say, stealing a peek, not wanting to let on I'm halfway interested.

"Why not? Really, the light blue would be perfect. See the ones I mean, with the seashells and the little beads knotted on the streamers?"

I take a mouthful of ice cream with strawberry sauce. The ribbons are pretty, and I *am* kind of curious how they'd look on me.

"So, you want to go in?" Kirsten asks.

"Well . . . I don't have any more money."

"I'll loan you some, then."

I glance at her. It's tempting, her acting so nice. Part of me wants to go along with it, just so she'll keep it up. But no . . . If I wore fancy barrettes, Danny and Jason would tease me no end. I'd rather just let them call me mophead.

"I appreciate it, but no thanks."

She sighs. "Okay, it's your hair."

Finally we head for the grocery store.

Boring, boring, shuffling up and down the aisle as Kirsten studies the small section of cosmetics, complaining that they don't have the brand of eyeliner she wants, taking an eon to choose one little bottle of fingernail polish. Big decision between Flaming Plum and Whisper Rose.

While she debates, I dig my free hand into my pocket for Jane's letter. Darn! My ice-creamy fingers stick to the tissue. I pull my hand out and try to lick them clean. Yech. Fuzzy bits in my mouth. I'm picking the gunk off my tongue when I look up and see a girl slink in next to Kirsten by the cosmetics.

I can't help staring. She's tall and thin, super tan, with long, white-blond hair that hangs down in permed squiggles. And her outfit . . . white boots, shorts, a black tube top and a denim jacket studded with rhinestones.

All that looks weird and out of place enough in the Perpetua Grocery Store, but the thing that really gets to me is this: In her hand she's holding—right out in the open—a box of tampons!

She just stands there like, yeah, I've got my period, and I don't care who knows it. I swallow hard. I just got my own period for the first time a couple months ago, and being reminded of it makes me feel funny. No way could I walk in a store and buy that stuff.

But she looks old and sophisticated, like she's been everywhere, done everything, and knows all about things

I don't even want to imagine. She's got to be at least seventeen.

By now Kirsten's noticed her too.

From the way Miss Weirdness is pawing through the makeup packages, glancing at them, tossing them back, it seems she and Kirsten at least have something in common: They both think the selection here stinks.

Awestruck, Kirsten shifts to give her room.

Now the white-haired girl takes a tube of lipstick out of the dispenser slot, pulls off the top, and twirls the stick. Then, peering into a display mirror, she draws it across her lower lip.

"Hey!" I blurt out. "You're not supposed to do that."

She turns, blinking pale gray eyes. "And why not?"

I can feel my face turning red as I stand there dangling the empty plastic ice-cream boats from my sticky fingers. I'm not sure why not. Laws about germs, maybe?

"What's the mirror for if they don't want you to try it on?" the girl says.

My mouth twitches in this horrible way it does when I'm nervous. I shrug.

The girl turns back and makes a kiss at the mirror. I guess she likes the color because she recaps the lipstick and takes it with her to the checkout.

Kirsten and I watch her pay for the tampons like they were jelly beans or something. Then she flips down her black sunglasses and heads outside.

Kirsten has this funny look on her face. "I wish I could be like that." She sighs. "All my life I've wanted that kind of charisma."

Someday I'll Laugh About This

Charisma?

Suddenly she turns on me.

"Why on earth did you have to go shooting your mouth off like that?"

"Hey, I couldn't help it. It just popped out."

"You're *always* doing that. Just saying whatever dumb thing you think of."

I hang my head. It's not the first time I've been accused of this. "It just didn't seem clean or something."

"She bought it, didn't she?"

"But what if she hadn't've?"

"But she did! Jeez, Shelby, I don't know when I've been so embarrassed."

"I'm *sorry,* okay?"

Pouting, she grabs a lipstick the same shade as the other girl bought and adds it to her basket of stuff.

The cabin's empty when we get back. I run down the stone steps into the old road. From the bluff I can see everyone on the beach.

"Hey, look! Daddy's got the rubber raft!" I race down and kick off my shoes at the spread-out blanket where Mom and Aunt Margo are reading paperbacks.

"How was town?" Mom asks.

"Fine," I call back over my shoulder. I'm halfway to the surf when Mom yells something about my bathing suit, but I just keep pounding toward the three whooping boys in the inflated boat.

"Make room!" I yell, splashing through the water and throwing myself into this floating tangle of arms and legs.

A big grin splits Daddy's beard as he holds the boat's rope, guiding it into the crashing white waves. We shriek each time the boat gets hit and hurled toward shore, Daddy slogging after us to catch the rope and tow us out again. We do it again and again until finally a wave catches us sideways, dumping us into the churning, knee-deep water. We jump up, squealing with cold and laughing.

I run toward the blanket, the taste of salt in my mouth and the sting of it in my eyes. I'm streaming water and shivering.

"Look out!" Mom says. "You're dripping all over me."

"Sorry." I step back, teeth chattering. This is Oregon, remember. The water numbs you. Our fun has to be fast and furious. You're either in the spirit of it totally or you get out quick.

"You better run up and change before you freeze," Mom says. "Then come back and tell us what Jane's got to say. Kirsten says you got a letter from her."

I clap a wet hand over my mouth and moan.

"What's wrong?"

I sag. "Nothing. Just this." I dig into the pocket of my soaking jeans and pull out a soggy wad of yellow toilet tissue. "And I didn't even get to finish it!"

I turn and stomp up to the cabin, leaving them with their what-now looks frozen in place.

Chapter Three

I'm down on the beach later that afternoon, skim-board-ing all by myself. Kirsten says it's too cold for her, and the boys are in a mean, no-girls-allowed mood. A fog bank's hanging over the ocean. There's no horizon. The gray waves seem to roll in out of the mist. I wait for the hiss as a wave pulls back out, then I spin the disk across the film of water that's left, jump on it, and glide. Usually this is fun, but today I'm just doing it in a who-cares sort of way. One slide after another, I work my way to the creek.

A mustard-colored steam shovel on the other side is piling huge riprap rocks against the crumbling banks, try-ing to stop the erosion. It reminds me of one of those mechanical dinosaurs we saw at the science museum, its long neck bending as its jaws clamp onto a rock. Then it swivels, creaking, and drops the rock from one pile to the other. The roar of the ocean muffles its engine, but the clang of steel against rock makes a weird echo in the fog. I hate how it looks there, ruining the naturalness of things. Even motorcycles aren't allowed on this beach, but here's this big hunk of machinery . . .

As I start back toward Sea Haven, I see old Mrs. Blake

Linda Crew

from the cottage just south, stumping along in her rubber boots, poking her walking stick in the rocks and driftwood up by the bank. She's picking up garbage. Having trouble, too, looks like. She can't bend over so well anymore.

We used to be so scared of her. We thought she was a witch. Once Jason called her the hunchback. Boy, did Aunt Margo ever chew him out for that. She said the lump on Mrs. Blake's back was some sort of disease and she couldn't help it. Of course, we all understand that now. When we go by her cottage on the bluff trail, she always waves us in for cookies. Mom and Aunt Margo say she still looks just like she did when they were little.

I roll the skim board hoop-style across the sand toward her. "Hi, Mrs. Blake. Want some help?"

She glances up. She's wearing this funny tweed hat with the brim turned down. "Well, sure. I guess some young bones would be of use here." She peers at me. "Now, which one are you?"

"Uh, I'm Shelby Graham, Steve and Nancy's daughter?"

She looks like she's expecting more.

"Dorothy and Bill Beyerlein's granddaughter?"

Still the look.

"John Jenks's great-granddaughter?"

None of this seems to ring a bell, which is strange. I thought Mrs. Blake had known our whole family for years.

"I guess you don't remember me," I say gently, sorry for her that she's getting so forgetful.

Someday I'll Laugh About This

"Huh! Course I do." She laughs. "I couldn't remember your name exactly, though, and then I kind of got to enjoying the way you were tracing yourself back, there!"

"Oh." I flush.

"And then you've got to realize you don't look the same. You've grown."

"I have?"

"Well, look at yourself, girl!"

I look down, but all I see is the same old rolled-up jeans and sweatshirt. I guess it's hard to see the changes when you live with yourself every day.

I push back my tangly hair and start pulling sandy ropes of plastic sacking from between the rocks and driftwood. It doesn't take long to fill her bag. All this junk the tide's brought in.

"Plastic," Mrs. Blake mutters. "Awful invention." She pokes her stick through one hole of a six-pack holder and yanks it up. "See this thing? Four hundred and fifty years this can last in the ocean, they say. And all the while it's choking birds, killing them. They even try to feed it to their babies." She shakes her stick at some unseen litterbug. "I'd sure like to have a word with whoever's dumping this stuff out there." She shakes her head. "No, beachcombing isn't what it used to be."

"Did you used to find real good stuff?"

"Oh, sure. Glass fishing floats from Japan. Bits of net. And of course, when I was a girl, we were still finding lots of Indian artifacts along the bluffs."

When she was a girl . . . With her wrinkled cheeks and the hump in her spine, it's hard to imagine she was

21

ever young. I can't picture it any more than I can picture myself old.

"Mom says that was all pasture along there."

She nods. "Cows chewed it right down."

"Must've looked a lot different."

"Our little house was the only one." She shakes her head. "Sat there s'pretty."

Now there are cottages all over the place. I look up at Sea Haven. It's the gray-shingled one with the green trim, just to the left off the old road.

Suddenly something occurs to me. "Mrs. Blake? Were you mad when Grampa Jenks built our place?"

A squawking laugh bursts out of her. "Lord, you're a funny child!"

Give me a break. Does everyone have to make fun of me?

She sees me flush. "No, no, that's fine. Your question surprised me, that's all. Most young people never seem to care what went on before."

I drop a faded, red Wisk bottle into the sack. "So, *were* you mad? About Sea Haven, I mean?"

"Well, let me think. You know, I've seen so many changes, it's hard to recall. I mighta been. I was something of a young hothead then. So maybe I was. But pretty soon I started seein' that I couldn't get all worked up over every new thing that came along. Why, I'd-a died of aggravation long ago if I got mad about every new cabin that went in along here."

"I like things to stay just the same," I say.

"Never do, though." She turns herself around and

nods toward the steam shovel down by the creek. "Nothing's going to stop the ocean from wearing away that bank, for instance. Oh, they might stall it, but in the end the ocean'll win. It's just the way of things."

"I'm sure glad Grampa Jenks was smart enough to build Sea Haven back where we wouldn't have to worry about that."

"Yup. Both our places, 'founded on a rock.' That's from the Good Book."

"You know, I think Grampa Jenks used to say that too. It sounds familiar."

"Fine man, your great-grandfather." She gazes out to sea for a minute like she's looking into the past, then she turns back to me. "You come from good stock."

I'm quiet for a moment, thinking things over. "So it's okay with you about the house on the point?"

She chuckles. "Well now, that's just a little bit different, isn't it? It hurt me to see that bluff go . . . all the wild strawberries. Used to be an old driftwood bench out there . . . we hacked it out of a log. . . ."

"I remember it!"

"Yes, well, it was right there that my Thomas asked me to be his bride."

"Really?"

She nods, her eyes watery. "Of course, it's not this man Dymond's fault I'm attached to the place. And he did buy the land from old McTeague fair and square." She cranes her neck up at the house. "Still, it's a prideful sort of place, isn't it?"

"My parents say they must be really rich."

"Hmmph. That doesn't give them any right to block off the road, does it?"

"What road?"

"Right there." She lifts a gnarly finger toward Sea Haven. "The old county road. Haven't you heard? Oh, that man has big plans. Claims the roadway's his now. Wants to put up one of those condominium things."

"You mean we wouldn't be able to walk along the bluff path to town?"

"Not if he has his way."

"But that's terrible! We wouldn't even be able to get to the wood yard."

"The wood yard?"

"Yeah. You know, your cove. That's what we call it, down the other side of the point where all the driftwood piles up?"

"Oh. Well, no. The way I hear it, that'd all be blocked off. I wouldn't be able to get down there myself—not that my old legs are too good for hiking on the rocks anymore, anyway."

"But still, he can't do that, can he?"

"Well, he's got a right to try, I s'pose." She blinks up at the house again, then turns to me. "And we've got a right to try and stop him. I've read on this. I know what's what. And I'm going to talk to a lawyer. We've all passed along that road for years. Testimony, that's what we'll need. Evidence. Don't you folks have any old pictures that might help?"

"I don't know." Then I remember something. "We do have sixty years of logbooks. I might be able to find something in those, something like, 'We walked into town today along the bluffs.' Would that help?"

"Might. Worth a try. You see, my girl, this isn't nature and time having their way. This is a piece of man-made mischief, and I don't intend to take it lying down." She winks at me. "You watch. You'll see. The only thing worse than a young hothead is an old hothead!"

Chapter Four

From my bed up under the eaves, I smell coffee perking down in the kitchen. Wood smoke too. Daddy must have started a fire in the big stone fireplace before he took off fishing on the Perpetua River.

I peek out from our snuggly nest of quilts. The boys are up and gone, their beds empty jumbles. I lean over Kirsten and pull back the window curtain with a scrape of rusty rings.

The sun is dazzlingly bright on the rows of white breakers. Wisps of fog drift over the sand. Someone's running down there. I squint. Aunt Margo.

Under the covers, Kirsten stirs. "You're crunching me."

"Sorry. Hey, let's get up. It's a great day out. The fog's already burning off."

She pulls a pillow over her head. "I wanna sleep in."

"Oh, come on." I pull her arm in a kidding way.

She jerks it back. "Leave me alone."

"Okay, okay." I swing my feet to the cold linoleum floor. "Have it your way." I pull on my jeans and sweatshirt and bound down the stairs, ducking to miss the beam. "Morning, Mom."

She's popping crumpet bread into the toaster as the boys troop in, wet to the knees.

"You kids!" she says. "Why can't you ever just put on your shorts or bathing suits first thing in the morning?"

"Well, *Mo-om,*" Danny says, "we never *mean* to get wet."

Aunt Margo bounds in after them. "Whew! That felt great. I'm going to have to get you running, Nance."

I glance at Mom as I take my place at the table. Fat chance. She looks totally unathletic in her faded flannel shirt, jeans, and Birkenstock sandals.

"I can't see pounding my bones into that hard sand," she says, handing me a fistful of forks. "Besides, someone's got to feed this mob." She slides fried eggs onto the plates.

"Oh, I'm sorry," Margo says. "I should have been up here helping you."

"Don't worry about it. You run, I'll cook."

"You cook and I'll get fat! Now Brandon, why don't you sit here by Shelby?"

Brandon jerks away as I scoot to make room. "No! I'm sitting on the boys' side." But as soon as he takes his place, he shoves his Transformer back across the table under my nose. "Guess what? I can do some *amazing* stuff with this. Now. Watch carefully. See, I pull his arm out here—"

"Not at the table, Brandon," Aunt Margo says.

"But just let me—"

"Brandon, that's enough!" Margo spreads her napkin in her lap. "Now . . ." She studies the faded map of the

28

world above Jason's head. "I'm thinking of a country that begins with the letter . . . *N.*"

"Narnia!" Danny shouts.

"A *real* country."

"Norway!"

"Nigeria!"

"Nicaragua!"

"We need a new map," Mom says.

"Yeah," I say. "Didn't this one used to have lots brighter colors?"

"And half the countries have changed their names or been overthrown," Mom points out.

But they'll never take it down. Nothing at Sea Haven is ever carted away until it absolutely falls apart. Anything that survives just sits here, year after year, turning antique. Just as well. Aunt Margo says the ancient wicker furniture she almost gave to Goodwill is back in style now.

Now Margo turns to Mom. "Mrs. Blake was down on the beach and I was asking her about the road—you know, this business Shelby came in with? I thought maybe Shelby'd gotten mixed up, but . . . well, Mrs. Blake thinks he's going to block it off."

"Oh, I can't believe he'd try that," Mom says. "I don't care if it is just a maze of tire ruts at this point. Legally it's still a county road."

"I'm just reporting what she said, is all."

Kirsten comes out in her hot-pink nightshirt, hair spiking up, eyes bleary.

"Breakfast, honey?" Margo chirps.

Kirsten shakes her head, turns and goes out through the kitchen to the bathhouse, just outside the back door.

I plop my chin in my hand. "What's the matter with her, anyway?"

"Shelby," Mom says, "that's not—oh, dear, watch out. Your hair's dragging in your egg yolk."

"Well, look at her!" I swipe at the gooey frizz with a wadded napkin. "She's like a different person this year. Just because she's got some dopey boyfriend . . ."

"I'm sorry, Shelby," Aunt Margo says. "Kirsten's going through a hard time right now."

"Girls get totally strange at this age," Jason mutters to Danny. "Just wait till *your* sister starts in."

"Well," Brandon says, "I have an excellent suggestion."

Excellent suggestion? This cracks me up. "Weird kid you're raising, Aunt Margo. Does he always use such big words?"

Aunt Margo nods in a spacey way, like Brandon's a constant surprise to her too.

He's really cute. He has these funny ears that stick out like radar receivers, taking in everything as his head swivels on his skinny little neck.

"If Kirsten's mean," he declares, "we'll just say, 'Go away, Kirsten, and stay away until you're ready to behave yourself!' "

"I wish," Jason says. "But when you're related to somebody, Brandon, you're stuck with them."

"Now come on, kids," Margo says. "This isn't such a bad bunch to be stuck with, is it? Remember what Gramma B. says . . ."

"Make things nice!" we all sing out, wagging naughty-naughty fingers at each other.

"Now don't forget," Margo says as we scrape back the benches to escape. "Before you start playing, everybody go down to the wood yard and each bring up as big a chunk of driftwood as you can carry."

"Aw, do we have to?" Jason lets the screen door slam as he drags back in.

"Yes, you do. You know the rule: one piece a day."

"This is supposed to be a vacation," Danny complains.

"It's our vacation too," Mom reminds him. "Just be glad you don't have to haul enough for the old wood stove, like we did when we were kids."

Danny and I trade looks. We've heard all this before—the kerosene lamps, the baths in the sink, the heated rocks to warm the cold beds. . . .

"That's right," Margo puts in. "We had to get *three* chunks of wood a day, and I don't remember us complaining. . . ."

"Yeah, yeah," Jason says, showing his braces, "and you came over the mountains in a covered wagon. . . ."

"And the snowdrifts were ten feet deep. . . ." I go on.

"Okay, okay, just get the wood."

An hour later the wood's piled in the shed and we're down on the beach. Daddy's back from fishing and sprawled on the old green army blanket.

Lying on my stomach, I flick sand into the breeze with my toe. Every once in a while I steal a peek at Kirsten. Amazing. Look at the way she fills out that bikini top. On second thought, don't look. I bury my head in my arms. This settles it—I'm not getting into my bathing suit the whole vacation, no matter how much Mom complains about soaked clothes. It's not that I'm a hundred percent flat—actually, that'd be better. What I've got are these little . . . bumps. Not enough to fill up a bra but enough to make a T-shirt look totally weird.

"Hey, come on, Dad!" Danny runs down the path and jumps on him.

Mom looks up from her paperback. "Don't do that, Danny. He's sound asleep."

"Dad? Dad!"

"He's not here," Dad mumbles.

"Da-ad! Help us get this monster kite up."

"Check this out, Uncle Steve." Jason holds up a plastic octopus with eight tentacle tails.

After they've dragged him off, I turn to Kirsten. "Want to play double solitaire?" I'm careful to keep my eyes on her face. "I'll go up for the cards."

She wrinkles her nose, shakes her head.

"Well, how about going down to the crick?"

"What for?"

That stops me. "I dunno." Since when did we need a reason? I wait a minute and try again. "Want to make a sand fort?"

She blinks with a run-that-by-me-again look.

"Well," I say, getting impatient, "what *do* you want to do?"

She adjusts the old green and yellow striped umbrella

she's hauled down to block the wind. "I want to work on my tan and read my magazines, okay?"

Wonderful. I flop back on the straw mat and roll to my stomach. Propping my chin in my hands, I watch Daddy and the boys with the kite for a while. The truth is, I'm not sure what I want to do, either. The next time I look back at Kirsten, she's doing one of those quizzes, making pencil checks in boxes.

I peer over her goose-pimply shoulder. " 'Do Others See You the Way You See Yourself?' Oh, that's great."

"Well Shelby, it *is* something to think about."

"Huh. Why take a quiz? You wanna know what people think, ask 'em. Ask me."

"Hey, look out." She moves away from me. "I don't want sand sticking to my suntan lotion."

"Oh. *Pardon me.*" I scoot back. I pick up another of the magazines and start flipping through the glossy pages. "These are so dumb!"

"Now Shelby," Mom says in a warning voice.

"Well, look at the goofy expressions on the models' faces. And their shirts hanging open and stuff. And the outfits they show . . . nobody in Corvallis would be caught dead in these."

Aunt Margo smiles. "Well, *Corvallis* . . ."

Mom stiffens up. "What's *that* supposed to mean?"

"Now Nancy, don't be so sensitive. Corvallis is a perfectly nice little town. All I meant was, it's not exactly a fashion Mecca, is it?"

"Thank heavens!"

"Here's a good one," I go on. "Says here to put egg white on your face."

Mom laughs. "Can't you hear them sitting back there in New York? 'What shall we tell them to do now? Pour milk in the bathtub? Wash their hair with beer?'"

"We *did* that, don't you remember?" Margo says.

"I remember you drinking it, is what I remember."

"And what about the oatmeal facial?"

"Oh, that was great! So disgusting, you *had* to look better when you washed it off!"

I guess I'm letting my feelings show because Mom looks at me and says, "Hey, it wasn't *that* bad."

Only it's not the idea of the oatmeal that's so hard to take. It's these long-legged girls with their dazzling white smiles. I mean, obviously *I'm* never going to look like that. I'm short and fat. Well, *I* think so, anyway. Dad says I'm just right—sturdy—but he only says that to make me feel better.

I turn to a picture of a bunch of girls playing around on a beach with some guys. They're really having fun.

"Totally stupid!" I say, tossing the magazine aside. I don't know why I'm talking like this. Maybe I don't want anyone guessing how much I wish I looked like a magazine girl that the boys get goofy over. I stand up. "I'm going out on the rocks."

"Okay," Mom says, then adds automatically, "Be careful."

I climb up to my special place, this little niche in the rocks that makes a seat just right for me. Sitting here, I can see south, all the way to Cape Perpetua when it's clear, and north as far as the earth curves. And to the west, nothing but ocean. Have you ever just sat and stared at the ocean? Mind-boggling, the way the waves just keep rolling in like that, crashing on the rocks, one after the other. And when you think how they've been doing this for millions of years . . . I sigh and wrap my arms around my knees. Makes me feel like my dumb problems don't matter one little bit. Not to the universe . . .

But they matter to me. And I'm bugged!

This vacation isn't what I was looking forward to at all. Kirsten and I used to have so much fun. When she still lived in Corvallis, we were almost like sisters. We stayed overnight at each other's house all the time. But now it's like she's changed and left me behind. And it's especially bad happening here. Maybe I never put it in words before, but I guess I've always thought of Sea Haven as a place where you could count on things staying the same.

Now it hits me that even my rock seat has lost some of its specialness. Before, it was private. Now the people in the new house on the point can look right down out of their big windows at me.

I get up and start back toward the beach.

I can't believe it. I just can't *believe* it. It's *her*, the weird-looking girl from the store, sitting on the blanket with Kirsten. Even from where I'm standing on the rocks I'm sure. There couldn't be two creatures with brown skin and white hair running around, could there?

Oh, brother. I make my way down the rocks toward

the group. How did Kirsten and this person get chummy so fast? You can see they've already been flipping through Kirsten's precious magazines together.

"Shelby," Mom says, "this is Tanya Dymond."

"From the house on the point," Kirsten adds.

Chapter Five

"We were just going to fix some lunch and show Tanya the cabin," Kirsten says to me. "Wanna come?"

"No, that's okay." This is really too much, meeting this girl after what happened at the store. And how come Mom and Margo are being so friendly to her when they're so upset about her house and what her dad might do to the road?

"Oh, go on, Shelby," Aunt Margo says. "You girls'll have a lot to talk about."

I roll my eyes at Mom and sigh. But in the end I shuffle after them.

"God," Tanya says the instant she steps into the cabin, "it's small, isn't it?"

"Well, yeah," Kirsten says, "but we're outside most of the time. . . ."

"But what do you do when the weather's crummy?"

What can Kirsten say? Admit that if it rains for more than a day and a half, we always end up in a big shoving match?

"And where do you all sleep?" Tanya asks.

"Well," Kirsten says, "there's two bedrooms downstairs for the grown-ups, and we all sleep upstairs in the loft."

"All? You mean those boys with the kite too?"

"They're our *brothers,*" I point out. "And it's a big loft."

"Wanna see?" Kirsten leads her up the steep stairs. "Watch out for the—"

"Ow!" Tanya cracks her head on the beam.

"Oh, sorry," Kirsten says.

"Honestly." Tanya rubs her head, looking around the loft. "Reminds me of the seven dwarfs' bedroom. I can hardly stand up straight."

My throat tightens. "I think it's cozy."

Tanya snorts. "Yeah, *cozy.* My dad loves that word. A favorite real-estate word for 'too small.' Of course, in Santa Monica, 'cozy' is almost a half million dollars."

"Wow." No use pretending I'm not impressed. "Mom says this place was built for only five hundred."

Tanya looks at the bare rafters. "I believe it."

"You have to remember," Kirsten says, "that five hundred dollars was a lot more sixty years ago."

"You guys have had this place for sixty years?"

"That's right," I say proudly.

"But why? I mean, didn't you ever want to trade up? Get something better? God, my father never keeps a property more than a year or two."

"Oh." I glance at Kirsten to see if all this is rubbing her the wrong way too. But no, she looks like a big-eyed doggy, lapping up Tanya's every word.

"You won't keep the place on the point, then?" Kirsten says. "I think it's really neat."

Someday I'll Laugh About This

Boy, if Mom and Margo heard her say that . . . !

"Oh, the house is okay," Tanya says. "But my father only built it so we'd have a place to stay while he's working on his condos. When he's done, he'll sell it." She glances around with a shudder. "I gotta get out of here. Gives me claustrophobia."

"Our house in Bellevue isn't anything like this," Kirsten assures her, following her down the stairs. In the kitchen she starts getting out cheese and crackers and cans of diet pop.

Tanya slinks around the main room, checking out the lamps and knickknacks with the same superior expression she had in the Perpetua Grocery Store.

"How old are you?" I blurt out.

"Jeez, Shelby!" comes Kirsten's voice from the kitchen. "Real polite."

"Fifteen," Tanya says.

"Really?" I'm thinking maybe now she'll ask how old *I* am, but she doesn't. She's looking at our big mosaic coffee table.

"Where'd you ever get this?"

"My grandmother made it," I tell her.

"Oh. I thought you must have gotten it at a garage sale or something."

"I think it's neat," I say, but now I study the table like I've never seen it before. It's a four-foot plywood disk covered with agates, a leaping tile trout in the middle, the whole thing bolted to cast-iron legs. It weighs about a ton. But it's a *beautiful* table. I chew my lip. Isn't it?

"God, I really miss California," Tanya says, checking

out the view from the window seat. "It's so dead around here. And no wonder. Look at that. One minute it's sunny, the next it's foggy. There's hardly ever anyone else on the beach."

"There's more people around than there used to be," I say. "Mom says they used to peel out of their swimsuits right on the front porch."

Tanya acts like she didn't even hear me. "There's never any boys. I mean, what's there to do? No TV reception, no cable for MTV, no radio except that one hick station. And the grocery store has what, ten videos to choose from?"

"You didn't tell me you had a VCR," Kirsten says.

Tanya shrugs. "About all it ever gets used for is my stepmother's preggo workout tapes."

"What's a preggo workout?" I ask.

"Stupid!" Kirsten says. "For pregnant people."

"Oh."

"Her stepmother's going to have a baby."

Tanya looks at me. "My dad's new wife is only twenty-three."

"Wow," I say softly.

"But let me tell you," Tanya says, her pale eyes suddenly flashing, "if she thinks she's going to use me for a baby-sitter, she can forget it."

Hey, she's *angry*. I was beginning to think Tanya never had any emotions other than being bored. Or does boredom even count as an emotion?

"I'm not kidding," Tanya goes on. "I hate babies. You couldn't pay me to have one. Ever."

"Really?" I haven't thought much about having babies myself, but still . . . I remember Brandon when he was tiny—his stick-out ears and big serious eyes, the way he'd pat your cheek. "How can you hate babies?"

"Well, some people hate dogs."

"Yeah, but people never used to be dogs. You used to be a baby yourself."

Tanya gives me a blank stare. "So? I didn't ask to be born." She seems so disgusted with everything, I get the feeling she's halfway sorry she *was* born.

"Is that kind of weird," I ask, "having such a young stepmother?"

"Well, how would *you* feel? It's even worse for my brother. He's nineteen. Didn't even want to be on the same coast with her, so after spring term finals, he split for Hawaii instead of coming home."

"Gee." I chew my thumbnail. "What happened to your real mom?"

"What happened to her? She got dumped, that's what."

"Oh." I thought maybe she had died or something.

"She hit forty-five and Dad hit the road."

"Just because she was forty-five?"

"Oh, who knows? But I think that's about the size of it."

"That's not very fair. Nobody can help getting older." I don't know why I'm sticking up for this woman I've never met, but what Tanya's father did bugs me too. I mean, is forty-five some magic cutoff age when men leave their wives? I think about my mom and dad. I sure hope not.

Nobody says anything for a while. Then Kirsten starts in on how deadly Sundays are.

41

"For one thing," she says, "no mail. And I'm expecting a letter from Troy, that guy I told you about?"

She means this to impress Tanya, but Tanya just looks puzzled. "So why don't you phone him?"

Kirsten glances away, picks at something stuck on the vinyl tablecloth. "We don't have a phone."

"No phone?" From the look on Tanya's face you'd think Kirsten just announced that nobody in the family had ears. "Why?"

"We've never had one." I lift my chin. "Our parents like it that way. They don't want a lot of junk calls about buying cemetery plots and stuff like that."

"Haven't they ever heard of unlisted numbers? I mean, what if you have, like, a medical emergency?"

I shrug. "There's no hospital or ambulance around here, anyway. If something happens, you just have to drive the person up to Newport or back home, so what's the point?"

"I bet they'll be sorry someday."

"Oh, I don't know. When our uncle Jack was a kid, he had an appendicitis attack here. If they didn't put a phone in after that, I doubt they ever will."

"So did he die or what?"

I suck in my breath. To even *think* of Uncle Jack dying . . . "Of course not. They got him to the hospital in time."

Tanya throws her white hair back and turns to Kirsten. "Well, you can use our phone if you want to call this guy."

"But it's long distance."

"Of course it's long distance. *Everything's* long distance from here."

"What I meant," Kirsten says, "is that I wouldn't have the money to pay you. I just blew it all on new makeup."

"No sweat. My dad never looks at the bill. I phone my friends at home every day—couldn't survive if I didn't. That was part of the deal when I gave in about coming up here. I told him straight that if I couldn't call Shawn every day, I'd probably get anorexic or something."

"Shawn's her boyfriend," Kirsten informs me.

"Oh." Of course. Well, Tanya *is* pretty thin. I can see where a threat like that might make her dad freak out.

"Want some pop?" Kirsten asks her.

"Whatever." Tanya takes the can and looks at it. "Don't you have any of the caffeine stuff? Oh, well . . ." She pops open the tab. "I'll get my fix later." Taking a sip, she starts checking out the family photo gallery on the wall.

"Who's the guy with the beard? Is he the one who took you guys out in the rubber raft?"

"Yeah, that's my dad," I say, edging in protectively. It gave me a funny feeling, realizing she'd been watching us.

"What is he? Some kind of hippie?"

"No, he's not a hippie. He's an air-pollution expert." Why was she so interested in my dad, anyway?

"But you haven't got any pollution here."

"We do in the valley. Besides, he works with fake pollution. He mixes up recipes of it. Denver smog, L.A. smog.

Like that. They put it in a chamber and check out what it does to leaves and stuff."

"How bizarre." She moves on to an old brownish photo.

"That's my mom and Kirsten's mom and our uncle Jack I was telling you about—when they were kids." I brace myself for a snotty remark.

But Tanya just studies the picture for a while, then lets out a long sigh. "I don't think my parents were into saving stuff like this." She moves away, settling into my favorite wicker chair like it's her throne, propping her crossed ankles on Gramma B.'s table.

I turn back to the picture. Strange. It's been hanging on the knotty-pine wall for as long as I can remember, but until now I've never paid much attention to it. Kirsten does look like Aunt Margo at thirteen. I wonder, do I look like my mother? I don't know, but people say we walk the same, which I guess means we don't mince along like some people. You know, girls who walk so carefully, like they must be worried every minute how they look to whoever's watching them. Mom and I walk like we're trying to get someplace.

And then there's Jack—special, wonderful Uncle Jack. In the picture he stands between his sisters, Mom and Margo, grinning straight at the camera while they kneel beside him, struggling to hold him still.

"You should see our uncle Jack now," I say, confident that in him we have something to impress even Tanya. "He's really neat."

I've always been crazy about Uncle Jack. He's like

44

magic. When he's around, the whole world lights up for me. I never talk about it these days, though, especially not to Kirsten. I've never forgiven her for crushing my daydream of someday marrying him, even if that was way back when we were little. I still remember how terrible I felt. "You dummy!" she said. "You can't marry Uncle Jack. You're related!"

Now she says, "Shelby's not kidding. Girls are always chasing him." Then she lowers her voice like she's letting Tanya in on a big secret. "He's in real estate too."

"No, he's not," I say. I turn to Tanya. "He fixes up old houses. Neat places with gingerbread trim."

"Well . . ." Kirsten flushes. "That's real estate, isn't it?"

Not like you wanted Tanya to think, I feel like saying, but for once I keep my mouth shut.

Kirsten's brown eyes narrow into mean slits. "By the way, Shelby, I almost forgot. Did you hear he's getting married?"

"What?"

"He's getting married."

"Come on, Kirsten, if you're just saying this to tease me . . ."

"No, honest. He told my mom."

Uncle Jack . . . *married*? Oh, I hate her for this— springing it on me in front of a perfect stranger, loading her voice with that fake innocence, as if she doesn't know perfectly well this will kill me.

"So he's a real fox, huh?" Tanya says. "Does he ever come around here?"

"Sure," Kirsten says. "Sometimes. Why?"

45

"I was just thinking how great it would be if my step-mother would fall for somebody like that and run off."

"Oh." Kirsten looks a little surprised. "Well, like I said, he's engaged."

"So? That wouldn't bother *this* wicked stepmother. If it didn't faze her that my father had been married for twenty-two years, I don't think a puny little engagement would get in her way."

"You're crazy!" I tell her. "Our uncle Jack would never get mixed up with somebody else's wife. Somebody else's *pregnant* wife!"

"You never know," Tanya says lightly.

I turn my back and look down at the beach from the window seat. The ocean's turned that pale green color it gets when the sun's filtering through fog. I'm mad at Tanya and mad at Kirsten and mad at Uncle Jack for getting himself engaged. Okay, maybe it *is* kind of excit-ing, the idea of being in on a wedding. But couldn't it be someone else's wedding? Because I'm going to hate shar-ing Uncle Jack, especially with some airhead girl who isn't even in the family.

I sigh. Why does he have to be my uncle? And so much older than me too? Because there probably isn't another man in the world like Uncle Jack. Who else could have discovered the fairy dust, for instance?

We were having a beach fire one night when he calls us from the darkness beyond the fire's light. "Look at this!" He kicks his foot through the sand and sends a shower of starry sparkles into the air. Amazing! We whirled for hours in the glittery sand, hating to stop.

46

Someday I'll Laugh About This

We'd never seen it before and we might never see it again. Daddy—always the scientist—says it was phosphorus. But to me it will always be fairy dust, and the one who made it happen will always be Uncle Jack.

Since then I've never been on the beach at night without scuffing my toe through the sand, hoping for the sparkles. . . .

"I've gotta get out of here," Tanya says now, jumping up, all restless. "Catch you later." She lets the screen door bang behind her.

I lift my head. "Good riddance!" I mutter. "And thanks a lot, Kirsten. I really appreciate you telling me about Uncle Jack in front of her."

"Oh, come on. What difference does it make who's around when you find out?"

"*You* thought it made a difference. Otherwise, why'd you wait to tell me when she was here? Why didn't you tell me before?"

"Oh, I don't know. I really wasn't supposed to tell you at all. Anyway, just because you're bent out of shape about it doesn't mean you have to be such a creep to Tanya. Especially after I had to make up all sorts of excuses for the way you acted at the store yesterday."

"Excuses for *me*? What about her? What about the way she was sniffing around here like it smelled bad or something."

"Well, it does. It's all musty."

"I like that smell. It's exactly the smell a beach cabin ought to have."

"Oh, sure."

"Kirsten, she was totally insulting. She acted like she was afraid of catching some icky disease in here."

"Well, it's not exactly what she's used to, you know. The house on the point even has a hot tub."

"I don't care if it has an indoor ice-skating rink! I think Sea Haven's the best place in the world, and she's got no right to act snooty about it."

"Shelby, be realistic. I like Sea Haven, too, but look at it. It's . . . well, it's shabby."

"Kirsten! I hope Great-grampa Jenks can't hear you right now."

"Oh, don't be dumb!"

Well, it isn't right, Kirsten talking like this. Not when our great-grandfather built this place with his own hands, hauled the rocks for the fireplace up from the creek himself. And there, on the beam Mom swears we'll never repaint even though it has a burned spot, he chalked a line by some old-time guy called Omar Khayyám: "And pity sultan on his throne." Mom says it means he felt like he was even luckier than a king, because even a palace can't top a place like Sea Haven.

And here's Kirsten, calling it shabby.

If this is how you get when you start growing up, I am not interested!

Chapter Six

When I see Mom and Margo coming up from the beach with Brandon, I run down the stone steps to meet them.

"Mom, is it true Uncle Jack's getting married?"

"What? Where'd you get this?"

"Kirsten just told me."

"Oh, Nance," Margo says. "I'm sorry. Darn that kid. I told her not to say anything. What happened is, Jack called on my birthday. First he lets me rattle on for twenty minutes, then the little smart aleck goes, 'Oh, by the way, I'm getting married.'"

"Well," Mom says, sounding hurt, "I wonder why he didn't call *me*."

"I thought he would. Of course I've been dying to say something myself, but I didn't think I should. It really seemed like his news to tell."

I follow them back up the steps, thinking how funny they are about Uncle Jack. They love to complain how Gramma B. always spoiled him, and they can do two hours straight on how irresponsible he turned out because of it. But in the end they're as guilty of favoring him as Gramma, and each wants to be the one he calls first.

Mom seems to get over her hurt feelings fast, though. "Lord," she says, "I can't picture Jack married. Our baby brother." She laughs. "But then our 'baby brother' is twenty-nine. I guess it's about time."

"After all the different girls who've wanted to marry him, it's hard to imagine who would finally be good enough for him. But then, Mom always did teach him he deserved the very best."

"Well, it'll be interesting to see exactly what he thinks the very best is, won't it? Has anyone met her? What's her name?"

"Kate, but that's all I know."

Kate. I just know she'll be beautiful. Suddenly it hits me. This is how life's going to be. The beautiful girls will always get the Uncle Jacks. They will even get the Jeremy Harrisons.

"Didn't you bring up your toys, Brandon?" Margo asks. She and Mom throw their beach chairs and blankets on the front porch.

"I'll get them later."

"Sweetie, with this fog rolling in, we may not get back down there today."

"I'll go back with him after while," I say.

When we're all inside, Margo glances around. "What happened to your friend, Kirsten?"

"Oh, she was going shopping up at Salishan with her stepmother."

"Stepmother?" Margo says.

"Yeah," I say, "her *twenty-three-year-old* stepmother."

Mom and Margo raise their eyebrows at each other.

"Hmm," Margo says. "Interesting."

I follow Mom into the bedroom. "Mom, what's charisma? Does that mean like being real beautiful or something?"

"No, not necessarily." Mom pulls a sweatshirt on over her head. "It's more like having a lot of charm. People who have charisma sort of draw other people to themselves. Why?"

"Just wondering. Do you think Tanya has charisma?"

"Oh." For some reason Mom looks like she's trying not to smile. She sits on the edge of the bed and thinks for a moment. "Well, I can't honestly say she has that effect on *me*. . . ."

"But Uncle Jack has it, right?"

"Yes." It comes out like a sigh. Mom smiles, then starts shaking her head at the thought of him. "Uncle Jack definitely has it."

"But with him it's because he's so good-looking."

"Do you think he is?"

"Well, sure. He's about the handsomest man I ever saw."

Mom smiles. "I think when somebody's as special as Jack, we see him as good-looking. It works the other way too. I knew a guy in college who could have been a model. He was such a jerk, though, it's amazing how fast you forgot his dimpled chin and wavy hair."

I slouch against the dresser. "I can't *believe* Uncle Jack's getting married."

"It'll be okay, honey. You'll see." She gets up and heads for the kitchen.

"But Mom? Something else I don't get. How come you and Aunt Margo were so nice to that Tanya? I thought you hated her father."

Mom stops in the doorway. "Well, honey, even if we don't like what he's doing, that's no reason not to be nice to her. It's not her fault, is it? Why don't you give her a chance? She's probably very lonely."

"But Mom!" My voice rises. "You should have heard her making fun of Gramma B.'s table!" I follow her into the kitchen. "She said it looked like something you'd get at a garage sale."

Margo hears this too. She and Mom glance at each other and start laughing.

"What's so funny?" I ask.

"Well, she's probably right," Margo says.

"Auntie Margo!"

Mom empties a plastic bag of bing cherries into a bowl. "As a matter of fact, we thought about adding it to the Saylors' garage sale down the street a couple years ago."

"You *didn't.*"

"Oh, yes we did." Margo pops a cherry into her mouth. "But the guys refused to move it. Your uncle Don says his back hasn't been the same since the day they carried it in here, and he's not about to carry it out."

"And your father blames his hernia on it," Mom adds. "Says the only thing it's good for is holding the house down in a storm."

"Hey, I don't think you should talk this way. Gramma *made* that!"

52

Someday I'll Laugh About This

Margo grins, showing her dimples. "It's so *cute* to hear Shelby defending that thing. Isn't she the one who fell and cut her head open on it the very day we moved it in?"

I touch the small scar that divides my right eyebrow. I never knew it was *that* table.

My eyes blur. "This would really hurt Gramma's feelings."

"No, no, now honey, look . . ." Mom puts her arm around me. "Don't you get all upset. Even Gramma B. admits that table is a far cry from the artistic masterpiece she'd hoped for."

"Actually, Nance, I'd say she's been a bit more blunt than that. *Monstrosity* is the word I've heard her use."

This is too much! Don't they have any sense of family honor?

I pull away from Mom and stomp out to the main room. Then I grab a pack of cards from the shelf and deal a solitaire game on the bumpy surface of Gramma B.'s table. Kirsten has her makeup collection spread out on the other side. In the window seat, Brandon's whispering the dead serious narration of his Transformer battle.

In a minute Mom comes in with a plate of fruit and cheese.

"This would be a great shade of eye shadow on you, Aunt Nancy." Kirsten the color expert. "Hey, I've got a terrific idea! Why don't you let me do a makeover on you?"

"Think I need it, huh?" Mom cracks a smile at me, trying to cheer me up.

Forget it. I don't want to. Besides—and this is a weird, guilty thing to be thinking—secretly I wish Mom *would* try a little harder, fix herself up like Aunt Margo.

"You could do Shelby," Margo suggests.

"No way!" I say. "You're not getting me in on this."

"Take it easy," Mom says. "You don't have to if you don't want to." Setting her mug of tea on the picnic-style dining table, she comes over and takes my face in her hands, tilting it toward the window's light. "But even if you're not interested in makeup—and, by the way, I think not being interested is just fine—you do need to wash your face better."

"I wash my face," I say, my unwashed face burning.

"Not well enough, though. You're getting a few black-heads." She starts to squeeze one.

"Hey, cut it out!" I swat her hand away. Why is she always picking on me, pointing out all my faults? Like a couple of weeks ago, hinting I ought to start using de-odorant. She might just as well have said, "Gee, Shelby, you stink."

"But what do you think, Margo? What if I just plucked her eyebrows a little bit? Here. And along here."

"Yow!" I press the heels of my hands to my eyebrows. "That'd hurt!"

Aunt Margo shrugs. "You know what Mama Jenks always told us. 'It takes pain to be beautiful.' "

"What a character," Mom says. "Your Gramma B. always claimed Mama Jenks never quite forgave her for

54

having us and making her a grandmother. That's why we always had to call her Mama Jenks instead of Gramma."

"That's dumb," I say. "A grandmother not wanting to be called Gramma."

"Well honey, it's not that she didn't love us. She just didn't like being reminded that she was getting older."

"Who does?" Margo says.

They're silent for a moment. A sad silence, it seems to me. Are Mom and Aunt Margo worrying about getting older?

I hate thinking about creepy stuff like this. Why can't everybody stay just as they are?

"Do you think it's true, though?" I ask. "That it takes pain to be beautiful?"

"Of course not! What was I just telling you?" Mom raises her eyebrows and adds loftily, "Beauty comes from within."

"Oh, yeah?" Margo says. "Well, when I'm on my sixtieth sit-up, the pain part still seems true enough to me!" She picks up a pink tube of roll-on cologne from Kirsten's collection, puts some on her wrist, and sniffs. "I think Kirsten takes after Mama Jenks. Remember her dressing table? Covered with jars of face cream, freckle bleach, powder, everything. . . ."

"I remember how she always lectured us on the sun giving us wrinkles," Mom says. "Of course, at the time we laughed."

"Ha ha," Margo says. "It's not so funny now." She gives Kirsten a pointed look. "That's something *you* ought to think about as you're turning golden brown, sweetie."

"How come those crinkles around Daddy's eyes can look good on him," I ask, "but they're not supposed to look good on women?"

"That," says Mom, "is an excellent question, and if you ever figure out the answer, you can write a book on it."

"Not hard to see who the little thinkers in the family are," Margo says, glancing back to include Brandon.

Great. Kirsten's the pretty one and I'm the smart one. And I'm smart enough to see that everybody thinks pretty is better. Take school, for instance. Lately the boys have started acting silly over certain girls. Which ones? Here's a hint: not the ones whose report cards they admire.

"Maybe Shelby could just start with combing her hair better," Kirsten says.

"Oh, shut up!" I sweep my cards together.

"We don't say 'shut up' in this family," Brandon warns.

"Well, look at it," Kirsten goes on. "A tangled mess. One of these days you're going to find a bird's made a nest in it!"

"And it'll lay eggs," Brandon crows, tossing aside his Transformer. "And one of them might break, and the goo will run down into your eyes, and you'll go, 'Help, help, I can't see!'" He staggers around, waving his arms, tangling with the wet legs of the jeans hung on the line above the fireplace. "'Brandon,' you'll say. 'Oh, Brandon, help me!'"

I catch my mother fighting hard not to laugh, and my face blazes. It's not fair! It used to be the kids against the grown-ups, or Kirsten and me against the boys. Now it's everybody against me.

"Actually, Shelby, your hair could be gorgeous," Aunt Margo says. "Lots of women pay fortunes to have their hair permed into curls like that. You and I are lucky it's in style now. When I was your age, I had to roll my hair on orange-juice cans to straighten it. And sleep that way!"

"Nobody made you," I say, slapping down a new card game.

"I keep threatening her with a haircut," Mom says.

"No way."

"What's the point of having it so long," Kirsten says, "if you don't want to take care of it?"

The point is simple: No haircut, no going to the beauty parlor.

"Okay, then," Kirsten says, "if Shelby's not interested, let me do you, Aunt Nance."

"Well . . . only if you figure you can have me completely made over before I have to start cooking dinner!"

Kirsten goes to work.

She holds up a pinch of Mom's brown hair. "You could have *this*, Shelby. You could have straight and limp like your mom and me."

Mom's hand goes to her hair.

"Don't worry," Margo tells Mom. "Kirsten's got the solution for that. Hairstyling mousse."

"Oh, great," I say. "You've got a moose that comes in with a blow dryer and a curling iron?"

"Where? I don't see any moose." Brandon tugs at his mother's sleeve. "What's she talking about?"

"Nothing, Brandon."

"But she said—"

Margo sighs. "Honey, trust me. It's not that kind of moose."

Kirsten rummages in her cosmetic case and pulls out a fancy gold spray can. She presses the plastic nozzle and a blob of foamy mousse forms in her palm.

"Hey, let me try that," Brandon says.

"Oh, no you don't." Kirsten holds the can out of his reach and whispers to Mom, "I always have to hide this kind of stuff from him."

"Dad lets me put shaving cream on my face," Brandon insists.

"Well, this isn't Dad's shaving cream." She heads for the kitchen and gets a paper towel to wipe her hands. "I bought it with my own baby-sitting money, so keep your mitts off." She goes back to Mom. "Now, before we do your hair, let's start with a facial. First . . . a nice mud mask . . ."

Brandon howls. "A *mud* mask!"

"Brandon," Margo says, "don't you have some toys to go collect?"

"Yeah, come on, buddy." I grab his arm and steer him out the door. "This is no place for us."

Chapter Seven

I love the way the sun feels at our beach, cool and pure. You never have to fry and get all sweaty. I like the beachy smell too. Daddy always kids me that it's the smell of things rotting—seaweed and shellfish—but so what? Somehow, mixed with the fresh salt air, it smells good.

Right now I'm sitting against one of our canvas backrests, shoving my bare feet through the warm, dry sand. I have my eyes closed, mostly because Mom and Aunt Margo say more interesting things when they think we're not paying attention.

"Will you look at that?" Aunt Margo says. "A whole truckload of bricks those guys are unloading. Nancy, do you realize the cost of that? They must be putting in a huge patio."

The house on the point again.

"That thing is all out of proportion to the other houses around here," Mom says. "It's ridiculous."

"I saw him get in that big car this morning with a briefcase. A *briefcase*. It's so strange to see someone here with a briefcase."

I take a sip of pop. Tanya's father probably doesn't

realize his every outdoor move is being framed in the lenses of the official Sea Haven binoculars.

"I have to admit, though," Margo says, "I can't wait for Kirsten to come back and tell us what it looks like inside."

"How come you didn't want to go, Shelby?" Mom asks.

My eyes are still shut. "They don't want *me* along."

"Maybe you're being too sensitive," Margo says.

"Well, anyway, who wants to spend the day playing with makeup?" I open my eyes just enough to aim what I hope is a meaningful squint at the sprawling house. I make my voice dark and ominous. "Or whatever they're doing."

I get the reaction I'm after. Mom looks at me closely. "What's that supposed to mean?"

I scan my brain for something bad to say. Then I remember. "I think she *smokes*. Didn't you notice the smell on her?"

"Well, anyone'd smell like cigarettes," Mom says, "living with a father who puffs away like he does."

Amazing what you can find out with a pair of binoculars.

Margo's gone back to flipping through her catalog. Folding a page over, she passes it to Mom.

"The dress in the middle? That would look great on you."

Margo and Kirsten—one of a kind. Always trying to improve everybody. But Mom's really studying the picture. Is she getting ideas, now that Kirsten's makeover on her was such a big hit? She actually giggled when Daddy noticed and said how nice she looked.

"I wonder . . ." she says. "Maybe I should try something like that, just for a change. You know, Margo, ever since that expression 'aging hippie' cropped up, I've worried. Is that what I look like?"

"Oh, don't be— Brandon! Get off that log!"

"But Mo-om—"

"I said get off. Now."

"But it's half buried in the sand."

"I don't care. The tide's coming in and it might get unburied. It doesn't take much of a wave to roll a log like that. If you fell behind it . . ." She trails off like she hates to put it into words.

"You'd get squished!" I yell, helping her out.

"Uh, thanks, Shelby." Margo glances at Mom.

Well, why be delicate? Mom and Dad never are with me. They're always telling me gory stories about people who got logs rolled over them. Every time it happens anywhere on the coast, they always read the newspaper article to me.

Margo raises her voice to Brandon again. "Now how many times do I have to tell you to just stay off them?"

"Okay, okay." He hops down and scrambles to the top of the sand mound the boys started earlier. "I . . . have . . . the power!" Then, mixing He-Man and Star Wars, he starts catapulting Darth Vader into the moat.

"Look, Mom. *Mom!* Now watch this."

He launches into his demonstration, but when Margo's eyes keep drifting back to her catalog, he starts in on me.

"You watch, then," he commands me. "Over here."

"Oh, all right." I push myself up. At least somebody wants me.

"Okay," Brandon says. "Now. Darth Vader's walking along like this, see? He goes da de da de da de da . . . Then he steps off the trick ledge and . . . *aaaaaaahhhhh* . . . he goes flying into the moat. Isn't that neat? Now let's try it again, okay?"

I watch him repeat this stunt several times, complete with the *aaaaaaahhhhhhh.*

"No, that wasn't a good one," he says nervously, glancing at me, afraid I'll lose interest. "One more try."

I'm beginning to get the picture about Brandon. What he really wants is a full-time audience.

I dig my big toe into the sand. "You know what's so super, Brandon? If you ever fall off a cliff, you'll know exactly what to say."

"I certainly will." He tries a slow-motion dive from the sand pile. *"Aaaaahhhhhhhhhhh!"*

In a way I envy Brandon. He still knows how to pretend. I think I'm forgetting. It was just last summer that Uncle Jack brought these special sand castle molds and we made a whole village. I remember playing for hours, making up stories in my head. Now I just don't seem to know how to do it anymore—not the story parts, anyway. And when I tried to get into sand castle making with Brandon this morning, I noticed for the first time that I didn't like the feel of sand under my fingernails anymore. I used to just dig right in.

Brandon runs out to the wet sand where Danny and

Jason are taking turns with the skim board. He tries to tug the disk from Danny.

I can almost read Danny's gestures. Be *reasonable,* he's trying to tell Brandon. You're too little, you'll get hurt, etc., etc. But Brandon isn't buying it. Finally Danny shakes his head and spins out the disk for him.

Brandon takes off after it, knees and elbows pumping. As his feet hit the board, it shoots out ahead of him. Arms flailing backward, his seat smacks the hard-packed wet sand, and before the boys can haul him up, a small wave washes over him. He staggers to his feet, howling above the ocean's roar. Arms dangling away from his sides, he slaps tracks toward his mom.

"Oh, dear," Margo says, cringing. She knows that his wet jersey is going to be against her sun-warmed skin in about ten seconds flat.

"I can't do anything!" Brandon wails, hurling himself at her.

Aunt Margo holds him, making a face to show what a freezing bundle he is. "Give it time, sweetie," she says. "Someday you'll do everything the big guys do."

"But I want to do it *now!*"

"Well, first let's get this shirt off you." As she tugs at it, Kirsten and Tanya came down the old road path. "Oh, good. Kirsten, could you run back up and grab him some dry clothes?"

Kirsten looks pained. "Why does it always have to be *me*? I'm not his servant."

"Kirsten! I—"

"I'll go," I offer.

63

"Well, thanks," Aunt Margo says. "That's sweet of you."

"I don't want to play on the beach anymore," Brandon announces. "Nobody'll do anything with me."

Poor Brandon. Being able to pretend isn't doing him much good. He feels as out of it as I do. I wonder, Does he ever wish he could go back to being the center of attention, back before he figured out he'd never be able to keep up, back when everybody was fighting for a turn at pushing his stroller down the beach?

"I want to go play at my Star Wars base I was making on the old road."

Margo frowns, considering.

"It's okay," I say. "I was going up to the cabin for a while, anyway."

No way am I going to stick around and get zapped by the negative vibes Kirsten and Tanya shoot off. Kirsten's learned fast, with Tanya as her teacher. *I deserve to be someplace better,* she can now say with just a flick of her goopy eyelashes.

"Well, okay, Brandon," Margo says. "I guess you can play up there as long as Shelby's around."

So I go up with Brandon and help him get changed. Then he runs out to the old road with a tin bucket full of all the Star Wars figures he inherited from the rest of us.

I follow behind, hoping to catch him narrating his stories. Even though Brandon loves an audience, his best performances are the ones he does in private. I creep across the grass and down the short path that connects the yard to the old road. I'm so quiet, I surprise a little brown bunny, who twitches at me, then darts into the salal.

I'm straightening up from my crouch behind the bushes when Mrs. Blake comes along.

"Whoa there, girl," she says, leaning on her stick. "You could give a body a heart attack lurking there like that."

"Sorry," I whisper. Actually she scared me too.

She collects herself. "Say, have you dug into those log-books yet?"

"I forgot." The truth is, it didn't seem so urgent after Mom pooh-poohed the idea of Mr. Dymond blocking the road. "But I will," I tell Mrs. Blake.

"I didn't like to bring it up to your mother down on the beach just now," she says. "Not with the Dymond girl sitting there."

I yank off a fistful of salal. "My cousin's made friends with her."

"Hmm. I gotta say it, that girl is downright spooky-looking. It's not natural—skin so dark and hair so light."

"She uses those tanning booths."

"Tanning booths. What's that?"

"You haven't heard of it? People lie down inside this metal box with lights that make their skin dark."

"Oh, go on! It's not nice to pull an old lady's leg."

"I'm not! It's the truth."

"Well, I never. Say, I'm heading up to make chocolate-chip cookies. Want to come along?"

"Sure, but maybe later, okay? Right now I have to keep an eye on my cousin."

Linda Crew

"Oh yes, the little fella down in the gully. He's having a fine time with that shaving cream."

"Shaving cream?" Uh-oh. "Um, excuse me, I better check this out." I tiptoe back toward Brandon's base, keeping behind the salal.

"You will freeze on the icy planet of Hoth," he's saying, marching the long-suffering Darth through something white.

I crane my neck. What's that gold can? Oh, no! I clap a hand over my mouth. Kirsten's hair mousse!

"This'll teach you, you crummy villain!" He squeezes out more long strips of foam and dive-bombs Darth with the old wooden plane.

Stop him, I think, but my hand stays locked over my mouth. I watch as Kirsten's mousse gets smeared over the rusty red dirt.

Then I scuttle back to the cabin and start pacing the porch. How am I going to pull this off? Make everyone believe I didn't know what he was up to without actually looking like I wasn't taking care of him?

"Aaahhhh! Heeelp! I'm falling into the snow!"

My mouth starts doing its twitching thing.

Uh-oh, there's Kirsten, starting up from the beach! I dart in, grab a magazine off the coffee table, and quickly sit down on the front porch.

In a minute she appears at the top of the stone steps.

I know I have this totally dumb grin on my face, but I can't help it.

Her eyes narrow. "What's with you?"

I act surprised. "What do you mean? I'm just sitting

66

here reading. I'm reading all about . . ." I peer at the magazine. "All about a big oil slick."

She keeps this suspicious look aimed at me as she goes into the cabin. She comes out with a can of diet pop.

"Where's Brandon?"

"Oh, down in the old road." I wave in the general direction of the Planet Hoth.

"I'm supposed to check on him." She ducks under the arching shore pine.

I gulp, desperately trying to concentrate on a picture of an oil-soaked bird.

"Brandon! You little brat!"

I wince, picturing Kirsten's sharp-nailed fingers closing around his little arm, dragging him up. If only I'd stopped him . . .

Kirsten marches him up to the cabin.

"I'm sorry," he screams, clutching Luke Skywalker. "I'm sorry, I'm sorry, I'm sorry!"

"You're going to pay!" she says. "I'm going to make Mom crack open your piggy bank."

"But . . . but I was saving up for a Transformer watch!"

"Tough! You knew better than to mess with my stuff." She turns on me. "For Pete's sake, why weren't you watching him?"

I hesitate an instant too long. I can almost see the light bulb flash over her head.

"Wait a minute! You *knew* what he was up to! That's why you were sitting here with that dopey look on your face, wasn't it? Well, you're gonna get it too. Both of you!" She shoves Brandon at me and goes flying back down to the beach.

"Oh, brother." I put my arm around him. He smells like mousse. We huddle on the front porch step, prisoners waiting for our sentences.

Later I almost get the feeling Mom and Dad think the whole thing is pretty funny, except maybe for one thing: It does say right on the can, "Keep out of reach of children." So they have to punish me.

Brandon and I are banished to the loft, me with orders to read to him.

"Can my bears listen too?" Rooting around under the covers of his unmade bed, he starts pulling them out. "This one's Harry," he says, introducing a much-snuggled looking fellow. "And here's Chris, and Charles, and Charles the Second." He dives under the covers. "Dixie? Now Dixie, you come out right now." He surfaces with a blue-velvet girl bear. "She is *so* cranky. I guess it's because she's a teenager." It takes him a good ten minutes to get this bad-mannered bunch settled. Charles the Second, it seems, refuses to sit next to Chris, and Dixie's still pouting.

"Sometimes at night," Brandon says, "they fight."

"No! Really?"

He nods. "So I say, 'Hey, you guys! You're supposed to be a family. Now make things nice!' "

"What if they don't mind you?"

"Shelby." He gives me a funny look. "I work them."

"Oh. Right." Boy, it's hard to keep up with him. I fall on my stomach across his bed and check the view from this window. To the south, over the low, wind-shaped shore pines, I can make out the shingled roof of Mrs. Blake's cottage. I sigh. No cookies today, not for us. . . .

"Okay," I say, propping Dixie back to sitting position, "what are we reading?"

Brandon pulls aside the striped skirt of the orange-crate nightstand. He's probably stashed a bunch of those Little Golden Books we've had at the cabin for ages. *Bambi, Snow White,* the one where Mickey Mouse's nephews are lost in the department store at Christmas . . . all of them torn and taped, the corners of the covers rounded with wear. He'll want me to read them over and over . . . yawn . . .

"Here!" He shoves a paperback under my nose.

I stare at it. *"The Shipwrecked Phantom.* This is what you want me to read you?"

He nods, faking a little shiver of excitement. "I'm really into mysteries."

Three chapters later Brandon says he's kind of glad he squirted out Kirsten's silly hair junk if this is the punishment.

"You read good, Shelby. Kirsten never reads to me."

I smile. Brandon's okay. At least *somebody* appreciates me.

"Shelby? I have something special I want to give you."

"Something for me?"

He nods. "It's very special and it's invisible. You can only get it from somebody who already has one." He pantomimes wrapping something around my waist and makes a click with his tongue. "There. Now it's on." His voice is hushed, reverent. "Your own personal Returnity Belt."

"Oh. Is that something from television?"

He shakes his head.

"Are you sure it isn't Eternity Belt?"

"No, no," he says impatiently. "*Returnity* Belt. It has magical powers to protect you."

"Gee, Brandon, I'm honored. That's real nice of you."

He blushes, then gets serious. "Now. You can wear it all the time, even when you're sleeping, because . . . *it's invisible*! Isn't that neat? But the very best part is that you never have to get a new one because it *actually grows along with you*! And it really does protect you."

"How can you tell?"

"Because of the evidence."

I laugh.

He gives me a tired look. "Don't laugh when I use big words. I hate it when grown-ups do that."

"Sorry." I press my lips together. Suddenly it seems very important to keep from disappointing him. "What's the evidence?"

"Well, Mom and Dad are always telling me to watch out, never turn my back on the ocean, don't stand on rolling logs, don't play with matches or something bad's gonna happen and all that. But . . ." His gray eyes go big at what he's about to reveal. *"Nothing bad ever happens to me!* So see? The Returnity Belt works!"

"I'll be darned!"

"Unless . . . well, there's one other possibility. Mom and Dad say *God's* protecting me. But . . . I just don't understand. If they think I'm protected, why do they keep worrying?"

"That's a real good question, Brandon. You think about things a lot, don't you?"

"Of course I do. And Shelby?"

"Hmm?"

"It's okay with me if you want to keep reading."

Chapter Eight

I write a long, gripey letter to Jane telling what a rotten time I'm having. How Kirsten's dumped me for Tanya and Danny's picking up bad, anti-girl attitudes from Jason. I tell her I only have two people who will talk to me —one's five and the other's eighty-five.

The days drag on, and I start to realize that nothing I can think of to say will ever impress Tanya or Kirsten.

Here's how it goes when I try.

Hey, guess what? Brandon caught his first fish!

So?

Mom says we can have a beach fire and roast marshmallows tonight!

So?

One time a guy fishing for perch drowned right off the point there—a wave knocked him off the rocks.

So?

Did you know the sun can give you skin cancer?

So?

I found a pearl worth a million dollars in a clamshell.

So?

* * *

Mom keeps telling me to be nice to Tanya.

"Why should I?" I say. "She's not nice to me. She hates me. She's always making fun of our family. Like we're a bunch of know-nothing hicks or something."

"Shelby. If she really felt that way, why would she hang around here so much?"

"I don't know. Just to bug us, I guess."

"Well," Mom says, "I can't help feeling sorry for her. Somehow I don't think she's as tough as she'd like us all to think."

Well, maybe Mom's right about that.

One day she wears this silver charm bracelet.

"Hey, can I see that?" I ask her, coming out on the porch. "I used to have one of those."

"Did you?" she says, halfway nice. She and Kirsten are sitting on the railing. She holds up her wrist so I can look at the little tennis rackets and ballet slippers and surfboards.

"I never had nearly this many charms, though."

Kirsten seems puzzled. She's probably always thought charm bracelets were for little girls. But as she follows Tanya's every gesture, it's clear she's quickly realizing her mistake. Charm bracelets *are* cool, her copycat brain is right this minute whispering to her. I'll bet my allowance she's already plotting to get one.

"My dad used to give them to me when I'd do something that made him proud," Tanya says.

I check out a dangling unicorn. "He's been proud of you a lot."

She nods. "Here's the one that started it." She shows

74

us a silver ladybug with red-enameled wings. "He gave me this and the chain when my ladybug project won a blue ribbon at the science fair. That was way back in the third grade."

I watch her finger each charm. Her face is softer than usual somehow. I can almost get a picture of how she must have looked when she was little, how her eyes would have lit up each time her dad surprised her with some new trinket.

"See this tiny book?" she says. "It really opens. This was for getting straight A's."

Here's where I blow the mood. "*You* got straight A's?"

"Don't look so shocked. I used to. All the time." Her face has hardened up again. "But that was before I figured out how useless school is. Besides, why should I get good grades for him?"

Kirsten and I exchange glances.

The bracelet tinkles as Tanya drops her wrist. "I don't even know why I put this on today. I hardly ever wear it anymore." Suddenly she undoes the clasp and dangles the chain of charms at me. "Here. Want it?"

I step back, shocked. "I couldn't do that. I mean, thanks, but it's . . . yours. It means a lot to you, doesn't it?"

"Not really."

"But I think you should keep it."

She shrugs, drops it into her windbreaker pocket. Funny, she doesn't offer it to Kirsten. Maybe she's afraid Kirsten would keep it.

* * *

75

The only time Kirsten really talks to me these days is at night in bed. Sometimes, whispering in the dark, she seems like her old self, the one I could share secrets with.

"I felt like such a hick when we first got to Bellevue," she tells me. "There I was, zero friends, and right away I knew my clothes were totally wrong. I had to figure out real quick what was cool and what was nerdy or I would have been out of it forever." She sighs. "There's so much more pressure up there. Sometimes I miss how things were before, in Corvallis."

"Maybe it's not because you're in Bellevue," I say. "Maybe it's just because we're getting older." After all, I know plenty of Corvallis kids who'd probably call in sick if their designer jeans weren't out of the dryer in time for school.

"No, I think it *is* Bellevue. It's gotten to my mom too. She's got to have the right clothes, go to the right restaurants. When I see her falling for it, I realize how pathetic it is."

On the other side of the loft, I hear the boys whispering. Then they laugh.

"No, you never!" Brandon says. "You're making that up."

"I kind of admire your mom," Kirsten goes on. "The way she doesn't care what other people think."

Doesn't she? "Oh, I think everybody cares. It just comes out in different ways. See, my mom's friends all wear jeans and handwoven vests. Even if she likes those dresses in the catalogs your mom's always showing her, she'd be embarrassed to wear one. You know, like her friends might think she's trying to change and act fancy."

"Hmmm. Kind of like how you're embarrassed to wear pretty barrettes?"

Bingo. I hadn't thought of it that way, but Kirsten's right. Jeez. What's the use of being able to figure other people out if I'm going to be so dense about myself?

"Why do you suppose people don't like other people to know they care?" I wonder out loud. Kirsten doesn't say anything, so I try to answer my own question. "Maybe because when people know you care, they can figure out how to hurt you."

"Yeah, that's it," Kirsten says. "You know, you really are pretty smart, Shelby. Wish I could put my feelings into words the way you can."

So sometimes it's almost like it used to be. But other times our talks just turn into arguments.

"Aren't you even a little excited you got your period?" she asks me one night.

I listen to the chimney cap creaking in the wind. "Not really. I think it's a big pain. What's so great about feeling yucky every month?"

"Isn't it worth it, though, knowing that now you're really a woman?"

"Kirsten . . ." I sigh. "That's ridiculous. I know that's what they say, but look at me. I am *not* a woman yet. They just tell you that so you'll get all excited and won't gripe about the hassle."

It's silent in the darkness for a moment—even the

77

wind has stopped. Then Kirsten says, "I think you have an attitude problem."

Finally I try to have it out with her about Tanya. We're on our way down to the P.O. again, the only thing Kirsten'll still do with me. Tanya's too lazy to hike anywhere.

"I just don't see how you can be friends with her," I say, walking behind her on the bluff trail. "Don't you even care about this place? Doesn't it bother you about her dad blocking off the road?"

"Mrs. Blake probably doesn't know what she's talking about," Kirsten says. "I'll bet she's senile."

"She is not!" I dart around her, talking as I walk backward. "And just say it *is* true. What if we couldn't walk along here to Perpetua anymore?"

Kirsten stops. "Well, of course I wouldn't like it, but it's probably not going to happen for years and years, and right now I have more important things on my mind." She passes me. "Like how I'm sick of trekking down here every day and never getting a letter from Troy."

Give me a break. If it isn't Tanya Tanya Tanya, it's Troy Troy Troy.

"Well, did you ever call him?"

"No, I didn't, okay?"

"Hey, I just asked. Polite interest, you know. You don't have to get hostile."

"Okay, I'm sorry."

I twirl the bag of leftover waffles I brought to feed the seagulls. "So . . . why didn't you?"

78

Someday I'll Laugh About This

"Shelby!"

"All right, all right."

But then, after a moment, she says, "Oh, I don't know," like she's annoyed with the whole thing. "I guess I was scared to call. What if he doesn't like me anymore? What if he's got a new girlfriend? I mean really, why hasn't he written by now?"

"Well, he said it'd be death to be apart," I remind her. "Maybe he's dead."

She winces. "You're disgusting."

See what I'm up against? No sense of humor.

Reaching an open spot in front of one of the motels, I climb up on a driftwood bench, stick my hand in the sack, and fling waffle bits into the air. A flock of gulls comes swirling around me.

"Good way to get a bird-poop shampoo," Kirsten says. I laugh. I don't care.

Kirsten watches for a minute, then she gets up on the bench. "What the heck. Give me some too." And she starts tossing crumbs.

Don't look now, but we're actually doing something together. For just a few minutes, with the squawking gulls flapping the air around us, it's almost like old times.

But when the waffles run out and we have to leave the gulls fighting over the last crumbs, Kirsten breaks the spell.

"Tanya says I should play hard to get. She says I should quit writing Troy, make him beg for me."

"Tanya says, Tanya says. You should hear yourself. You act like she's the last word on everything." I stuff the empty sack into the can at the public wayside. "What is it you think's so great about her, anyway?"

"I don't know. I'm not into analyzing everything like you are, okay?"

"Is it the way she looks?"

"Well, sure, I guess that's part of it."

"But Kirsten, you're prettier than her any day."

She stops and looks at me. "Do you really think so?"

"Well, yeah." Suddenly I feel shy. "You are."

"Thanks for saying that, anyway." She straightens up, like maybe she's hoping I'm right. "But it's not just how Tanya looks. She's really smart too."

"That's not what you like about her, though. Even if it's true. Which I'm having a hard time believing. I wonder if she lied about getting good grades."

"She reads grown-up books. I've seen them."

"She does?"

"Yeah, she does. You know, Shelby, you'd be the first one to say we shouldn't judge somebody by looks alone."

"Okay, okay, but you have to admit, if she's some great brain, she sure does a good job hiding it."

"Maybe she wants to. I hate to break this to you, Shelby, but once you hit junior high, being smart isn't necessarily so great."

I scowl. Why is it when people use that tone of voice and say they hate to break something to you, what they really mean is they are thoroughly enjoying it?

"Frankly," Kirsten goes on, "boys aren't really interested in girls who're smarter than they are. If you're re-

ally smart and you want a boyfriend, you'll probably quit getting the top grade on every single test."

"That is totally stupid."

"I'm not saying it's right. I'm just saying that's how it is."

"Yeah? Well, someday I'll have a boyfriend, and guess what? He'll be smart enough to *want* a smart girlfriend!"

I'm not sure I believe this, but I like the way I sound saying it.

We walk for a while without talking, then Kirsten says, "Maybe I admire her because she's the first person I've ever known who really doesn't give a rip what other people think."

I don't believe that, but why argue? It's just a feeling I have. Something about her being so desperate to show she *doesn't* care. So desperate she'd even risk losing her bracelet to prove it . . .

"I honestly don't think she's afraid of anything," Kirsten says.

"She's reckless, is what she is. Like when you guys were playing chicken down on the rocks, not running away from the waves until the last second . . ."

"Yeah, why'd you have to go tell on us, anyway?"

"Kirsten! I didn't want you to fall in the ocean."

"Huh. I think you were just jealous because we were having fun."

"No, sir! I was scared you'd slip."

"But we didn't," Kirsten says. "That's the thing. It's like, you've got to live on the edge, give life some thrills. Can't you understand that?"

"No, I can't." Why would somebody want to run around doing things that could land them in the hospital? Or worse.

Looks to me like Tanya's begging for something bad to happen.

But Kirsten's had enough of hashing this over. I don't get anything else out of her until we reach the P.O.

"Oh, wow! Finally!" Kirsten presses the long-awaited letter to her breast and looks up like she's thanking God. Then she studies her name on the envelope again. "I can't *believe* it. I was beginning to think this would *never* come!"

"We really lucked out today." I sit down beside her on the post office steps with another letter from Jane, and also one from Uncle Jack.

"I can't stand it." Kirsten caresses the envelope. "Part of me wants to rip into this and part of me wants to take it real slow and make it last."

I open mine, eager to read. "No toilet paper this time." In a weird way it always cheers me up to read Jane's exaggerated stories about everything that's going wrong with *her* life.

I start in. Strange. Not the usual letter. For once, not much seems to be wrong in Salina, Kansas. Jane met a girl on the next block and they went to the new mall together. This Jennifer person also took her to a neat place called Frank's Fun Center, where kids show their report cards and get video-game tokens for each *A*. Lots of boys hang out there too.

Someday I'll Laugh About This

How come I have this odd little twinge of disappointment? I tuck the cheerful, boring letter back in its envelope. What's the matter with me? Don't I want Jane to be happy? Don't I want her to get used to Kansas?

I peek over Kirsten's shoulder. "All got rowdy at the Mariners game with some guys from . . ." That's all I can read before she folds it up.

"Well?" I say.

"Well, what?"

"You aren't exactly swooning. What's he say?"

Kirsten shrugs. "Just stuff. Nothing much." She takes out a comb and drags it through her hair a few times. "It wasn't exactly what I was expecting."

I look out over the little town to the place where the Perpetua River flows out into the ocean. "You know something, Kirsten? You've been looking forward to that letter so much, I'll bet nothing he could have written would have been good enough."

She gives me this sideways glare. "Don't you ever get tired of trying to figure everything out?"

"Yeah," I say. "Actually, I do." I sigh. Then I open the other envelope with my thumb. "Let's see what Uncle Jack says."

Kirsten gets up, sticks her comb in her pocket. "Read it while we walk back."

I scan the scrawl across lined notebook paper. "Listen to this! He's bringing that girl he's going to marry here to meet us! *Sunday.*" I check the traffic and follow Kirsten across the highway. "Wow. Can you believe it? I still can't picture Uncle Jack with a wife. I guess she'll be our aunt, huh?"

Kirsten nods, her black eyebrows pushed together. "She must be gorgeous. I mean, if this is the one he's finally decided is the best of all of them . . . Remember that girl the summer before last? What was her name?"

"I don't remember."

"Me neither, but I sure remember her blond hair. Tons of it."

"What I remember," I say, "is that she was always fussing with it and complaining that the damp air made it curl wrong. And I remember you putting seaweed in her sleeping bag."

Kirsten laughs. "It was your idea."

"But you actually did it." Hard to believe now. Two years ago Kirsten, in her long ponytail, was a different kid.

"I was really glad when he broke up with her," I say.

"What about that Cynthia? The one with all the clothes and the long fingernails."

"I didn't like her, either."

"You wouldn't like anyone Uncle Jack liked. You're just jealous."

"I am not," I lie. Of course I'm jealous! Uncle Jack always makes me feel like someone special. Even when he calls me Funny Face it's okay, because I can tell he likes me. And I like him just the way he is. If he gets married, he might change.

"Anyway," I say, "you feel exactly the same way about him. You know you do."

Kirsten flushes. "Well, I can't help it. He's just . . . he's . . ."

I sigh. "Yeah, I know."

Suddenly it hits me. Uncle Jack is coming!

Something else hits me too. I have to get out of this awkward stage. And fast.

I admit it, okay? I want to be beautiful. Beautiful and charming. Someone even Uncle Jack wouldn't *dream* of calling Funny Face. If possible, I want charisma. Would a day or two be long enough to make a spectacular change?

"Kirsten, you've got to help me. Remember when you wanted to do a makeover on me but I wouldn't let you?"

"Yes . . ." she says warily.

"Well . . ." I draw myself up. "I'm ready."

Kirsten starts walking again. "I don't know, Shelby. The way you've been acting lately . . ."

I follow her. "What do you mean?"

"Oh, come on." She starts ticking off my offenses on her fingers. "You put down everything I think is important. You make fun of me for missing Troy. You're always making snide remarks about my magazines. It's just like you said the other night—you found out what I care about and you use it to get to me."

"Gee, I didn't mean to hurt your feelings."

"Well, you do. Talk about *me* being weird this year. What about *you*?"

I sure can't deny this stuff. What surprises me is that it actually registered with her. I didn't think anything I said mattered.

"I'll be nice," I promise. "Just give me another chance with the makeover. Please?" Because as much as I've resented it, her secret, grown-up knowledge about makeup and everything is just what I need now to change my life.

"Well . . ." Kirsten stops on the trail in front of me and turns around.

"Okay. But I think we should get Tanya in on this."

"Oh." I hang back. "Couldn't *you* just do it?"

"I could, but I really think she'd have some good ideas, Shelby."

"Okay. One thing, though. No eyebrow plucking, okay?"

"Don't worry, Tanya says the natural look is what's in for eyebrows."

"Good!" For once I'm glad to let Tanya be the authority.

"But you have to promise to be cooperative. No acting silly. I mean, so help me, Shelby, if you embarrass me one more time . . ."

Chapter Nine

My eyes bug out as Tanya leads me and Kirsten into the biggest bathroom I've ever seen. A mini-gym's more like it. A bathtub as big as a small pool in the middle, and in one corner an exercise bike and one of those weight-lifting machines with all sorts of bars and pulleys. I stare at the gold faucets on each of the two sinks. *Gold.* Weird, though—one has a blob of toothpaste on it, and strands of wet hair are plastered to the sink bowls. I guess fancy doesn't have to mean clean.

"Sit here," Tanya orders me, scooping up the lingerie from a cushioned seat and tossing it on the floor.

I perch on the patch of pink velvet, glancing away from my reflection in the light-bulb-bordered mirror. Instead I focus on the litter of makeup, wadded tissues, and pop cans covering the broad counter.

"I brought my makeup to use," Kirsten says, pushing some of the stuff aside to make room for her flowered bag.

"Whatever," Tanya says.

She's studying my face in a way that makes me squirm. Already I'm wishing I had the nerve to bolt for the door. I can't even breathe in here, for Pete's sake. The room's too warm, and the air's thick with perfumey lotions and cigarette smoke. Reminds me of beauty parlors and how much I hate them. After that one visit in the fifth grade I promised myself—never again. But here I am. I couldn't feel much worse if they'd wheeled me into an operating room.

I shut my eyes, take a deep breath, and try to think of Uncle Jack.

"The first thing we ought to do," Tanya says, "is cut that hair."

I jerk like I'm going to jump off the stool.

"Oh, cool your jets," she says. "Haircuts aren't my thing, anyway. We'll have to settle for a good shampoo and conditioning."

"I could do some neat braid things," Kirsten says, taking a fistful. "I've been dying to get my hands on this."

The next thing I know, my head is being held over the sink and knocked against the gold faucets. Knuckles are kneading my sudsy scalp.

"Ow! Hey, take it easy!"

The comb-out's no picnic, either, each of them raking through snarls on opposite sides of my head.

It takes pain to be beautiful. . . .

As they work, Kirsten and Tanya analyze my features, discuss what they'll try, which shade of eye shadow will look best, whether to use liquid eyeliner or pencils.

"Her cheekbones are nothing to brag about," Tanya says, smearing on some kind of flesh-colored base, "but at least nothing's terribly out of proportion."

They talk about me like I'm not here. The only thing

they say directly to me is stuff like "Close your eyes, purse your lips, turn your head. . . ." I try hard to do what I'm told, hoping that somehow the results will make this torture worth it.

Then I get a glimpse of myself in the mirror. Hey, it *is* working. The liquid base hides some of my freckles, and the mascara makes my eyes look bigger, kind of dramatic. In thirty minutes they've added two years!

More eye shadow here, more rouge there. Kirsten and I exchange a glance. She's impressed too.

Finally Tanya throws down the blusher brush. "I need a break. Do you two want something to drink?" Without waiting for an answer she goes off.

I whisper to Kirsten, "What do you think?"

"It's great!"

"You don't think she's putting on too much?"

"No, it's terrific. Like one of those magazine makeovers."

I take a shy peek at myself in the mirror. Is that really me? Can a person actually grow up in one hour?

Tanya comes back. In one hand she has a can of beer. In the other, two more dangle from a plastic six-pack ring, clanking together as she swings them onto the counter.

I flash surprised eyes at Kirsten, expecting the same back.

But she's trying to be cool, like people are always offering her beer. She won't look at me as she pulls the can from the ring and pops it open. Then she actually takes a sip! Look at her, trying so hard not to make a face.

"Don't you want a brew?" Tanya asks me.

"Uh, no thanks." I'm still watching Kirsten. She's playing it awfully cool. Who knows? Maybe this isn't the first time she's tasted beer.

Then I notice this young woman standing in the doorway. Must be Tanya's stepmother. She's wearing an oddball maternity outfit that looks like somebody splattered black and white paint all over it. She has red socks, red lipstick, and a red scarf tied into a puffy bow around her ponytail.

I glance at the beer and swallow hard. Now we're in for it.

But Tanya's stepmother doesn't even blink at the cans, doesn't even seem to notice me and Kirsten.

"I'm taking my nap now," she says. "No loud music, okay?"

Tanya grunts.

"I was still asleep when your dad left. Did he say when he'd be back?"

"He said we'd see him when we see him. He might be in Newport all day trying to straighten out the road deal."

Tanya's stepmother yawns, pushes off from the doorjamb, and pads down the thickly carpeted hall.

"Nap." Tanya spits out the word. "That's all she does. The human incubator."

But I'm not thinking about Tanya and her stepmother. "What's this about a road deal?" I say.

Kirsten laughs. "Shelby's got this bizarre idea your dad's going to block off the old road."

"He is," Tanya says matter-of-factly.

Someday I'll Laugh About This

Kirsten's face falls. "He is?"

"I *told* you," I say under my breath.

"Well, of course." Tanya takes a long pull on her beer. "This condo is going to be very exclusive. You can't have everybody and his dog walking across the bluffs here."

I choke back a smart remark. I did promise Kirsten I wouldn't embarrass her. Besides, I'm busy getting used to my new self in the mirror.

Tanya aims the blow dryer at my half-dry curls. "You guys might as well face it," she says, raising her voice over the dryer's hum, "you can't stop growth. My dad says it's only a matter of time before this is all built up. Of course, it'll never be as good as California—too cold. But you'll see. Pretty soon there'll be condos all along here."

Well, it's sort of strange. She's talking about wrecking the place we love, and I know if she'd said this a few days ago, I'd have felt like jumping up and wrapping the dryer cord around her skinny neck. But right at the moment she's got me under her spell. All I can think about is my thrilling makeover.

Kirsten pulls my hair to one side and begins braiding. Meanwhile Tanya starts in on the beer I turned down, gulping it as she watches.

"Well, what do you think?" Kirsten asks me when she's done.

"Fine." Actually I think I look terrific, but saying so might sound kind of conceited.

"I hope you watched carefully how we did everything," Tanya says, "so you can do it yourself." Then she turns to Kirsten. "I think it's an incredible transformation. Don't you?"

Kirsten shakes her head like she still can't believe it.

"You're really cute, Shelby," Tanya says. "I'll bet you're going to be a knockout someday."

"Really?"

"Oh, definitely. Hey, you sure you don't want some beer?"

I'm blushing and feeling a little silly. "Well . . . maybe just a sip."

Kirsten grins approvingly.

I take the nearly empty can Tanya hands me. I don't really want it, but they're acting so happy with me, I hate to blow it. Yuk, the taste! How could anyone ever get drunk? Still, I giggle, surprised how good it feels to be a little bit bad.

Tanya talks to Kirsten's reflection. "Why don't we go show her off?"

I blink my glamorous eyes. "What do you mean?"

Tanya tosses the empty beer can at the wastebasket, missing. "Let's go up to Bayport."

"All right!" Kirsten says.

I flash on this picture of the three of us in the backseat of Tanya's stepmother's silver rental car, streaking up Highway 101. Hey, I could go for that. Being included sure does beat being left out.

Tanya starts checking her own makeup. " 'Bout time we broke loose from here, don't you think?"

"Yeah!" Kirsten says, starting to brush her hair. "Maybe we could even find some boys."

Someday I'll Laugh About This

"Boys?" I echo. I can see us now, coming out of the grocery store with our ice-cream bars. Three boys are lounging on the wooden bench by the watermelon bin. They whistle at us— No, that's dumb. . . . Maybe they just say something. But what? Maybe, "Hey, you from around here? Want to walk down to the bay?" Whatever. The point is, I'm with Kirsten and Tanya, looking cool, tossing my braids like I know my way around. The boys don't even realize I'm younger.

"So," Kirsten says. "How long does your stepmother usually nap?"

"Oh, hours. We'll be there and back before she even knows it."

Kirsten lowers her hairbrush. "No, I meant . . ." She hesitates. "She won't be driving us?"

"Are you kidding?" Tanya says. "What fun would that be? I'm gonna drive."

"But . . ." I glance at Kirsten. She can't pretend she's not shocked by this. She has to back me up. I turn to Tanya. "I thought you said you were fifteen."

"Yeah, so?"

"So you don't have a driver's license."

"But I have a learner's permit. I know how to drive. And I don't look fifteen, right?"

I sigh, the vision of us in Bayport fading. "Our parents would never let us."

Tanya laughs. "Well, I wasn't expecting you to *ask* them, dummy."

I look at Kirsten. She's chewing the lipstick off her lower lip, thinking hard. Then she blurts out, "We could tell them we're walking into Perpetua again. They'll never know the difference."

"Kirsten! You'd lie?"

"Come on. It's not really a lie."

"It's not? How do you figure?"

"Oh, Shelby . . ." With no good answer to this, all she can do is wave me away. Great. A minute ago I was their little darling, suddenly I'm back to mosquito status.

I just stand there, staring at their backs. They're really going to get in a car and drive seven miles down the road?

"No!"

They turn around and stare at me.

"I'm not going."

Tanya shrugs. "Okay, so don't."

"And you're not either, Kirsten."

"Says who?"

"Says me."

"How you gonna stop me?"

Heat rushes to my face. "I'll tell."

"You better not!"

"Kirsten, she was drinking *beer*! You don't drink beer and then drive a car."

"A couple of beers," Tanya says. "Big deal. It takes a lot more than that to get me drunk. Do I look drunk?"

She's got me there. I don't even know for sure what drunk looks like in real life. "Even if you're not drunk, you're still only fifteen."

"Good grief," Kirsten says. "How did you get to be

such a party pooper? Don't you ever want to have any fun?"

Of *course* I want to have fun. Does she think I enjoy being miserable and out of it and younger than they are?

"And really," Kirsten adds, "what a lousy way to show your gratitude."

"Hey, I'm grateful, okay? That doesn't make driving to Bayport a good idea. You think our parents would buy that as an excuse? We drove to Bayport with Tanya because she did a good job on my makeup?"

"Well, nobody's going to make you go," Tanya says as she rummages through her stepmother's purse for the car keys. "I didn't realize you were so scared of your parents. What can they do to you, anyway?"

"Well," Kirsten says, "I'd be grounded."

"Yeah?" Suddenly Tanya's giving us that weird-interest look again. "What about you?" she says to me. "What happens when you get in trouble?"

"She never *gets* in trouble," Kirsten says.

"I do too!" I protest. "I'd probably be grounded so fast . . ."

My folks are big on making the punishment fit the crime. Like if I borrowed the batteries out of Danny's race cars without asking and used them up, I'd have to buy him new ones. Or if I mouthed off and hurt someone's feelings, I'd have to apologize.

But I've never done anything big and bad enough to get myself grounded. And Kirsten knows this. Why does she have to make me feel like it's a terrible blot on my record or something?

"Come on, Kirsten," Tanya says. "Let's go."

Kirsten doesn't move. She looks at Tanya, then at me. I can see her jaw working as she grinds her teeth, trying to decide if the fun is worth the risk that I might blab.

Tanya jingles the car keys. "I'm not going to stand here all day. I'm leaving."

"Wait," Kirsten says, following her down the hall and out the front door. "I want to go, but if she's going to tell . . ."

I hurry behind. I just can't let her do this.

Tanya looks from Kirsten to me. "You know, I think you two kiddies deserve each other." She slides in behind the wheel of her stepmother's sleek silver car. "Why don't you go see if Daddy'll give you a little boat ride in the waves or something?" Then she slams the door and backs out with a roar, banging over a garbage can. She lurches the car forward, backs out again, and takes off.

Kirsten turns on me. "You reject!"

I start picking my way across the unfinished patio. I have to get out of this place, get back to Sea Haven.

Kirsten's right on my heels. "I mean, thanks a lot. I love the way you always wreck everything. Now Tanya thinks I'm as big a baby as you."

I turn and face her. "Kirsten, what if I *didn't* try to stop you and you got killed in a wreck? I'd never get over it. And think how mad at me everyone would be."

"Oh, don't try to make it sound like you're so noble when really you're just chicken. You're *afraid* to go to town with makeup on."

"I am not! I wanted to go. I really did."

"No, you didn't. You know what I think? I think you're afraid to grow up!"

Afraid to grow up. That hits home.

"Maybe I am," I say, hating the quiver in my voice. "But that doesn't make it right, what you wanted to do."

Kirsten grabs my arm. "I'm never going to forgive you for this. I stuck my neck out for you because you begged me. And you promised you wouldn't embarrass me, and now look at you. You're such a baby!"

I yank my arm loose, my throat aching with that ready-to-cry feeling. Head up, lips pressed tight, I hurry down the Dymonds' steps into the old road.

Oh great, Danny and Jason, coming down Sea Haven's stone steps on the opposite side.

"La-di-da!" Danny singsongs. "Look at Shelby."

"Shut up!" I march across the old road toward them. Maybe I'd been right. Maybe Tanya *had* gone a little overboard with the makeup.

Jason smirks, blocking the steps as I try to pass. "Kind of early for trick or treat, isn't it?"

I collar him. "I said *shut up!*"

"Whoa," Jason says, freeing himself, pleased no end to see he's gotten a rise out of me. "Look out, Danny. I told you she'd go loony when she started getting boobs."

Danny snickers.

That does it. I lunge at my brother.

"Hey, what the—"

I drag him off the steps and into the sandy dip of the old road, pinning him to the dirt.

"Yow!" He's got me by the braids. We roll over and over. I can hardly see him . . . stupid tears . . .

"The hold!" Jason yells. "Use that hold I showed you."

"Oof." My mouth hits the ground. I taste bloody dirt. My cheek drags over the grit. So much for makeup. . . .

Stronger than the last time we wrestled, Danny still ends up on the bottom. He's crying too.

"Come on!" Jason shouts at him. "You gonna get beat by a girl?"

"Stop it!" somebody's yelling. "You kids stop that right now!"

Panting, I ease off just enough for Danny to wriggle out. A mistake. Right away he has me down, my hair in the dirt, his orange-pop breath in my face. I kick like crazy, flinging up dirt that rains down on us. *I'll teach you to laugh at me.* I wrench my wrists free and push him up. Then I shove him down and sit on his stomach.

"Shelby Lynn Graham!"

I feel myself being dragged up by my father. His beard's against my cheek as he pulls me away from Danny, who lies there sniveling, a sandy stream of snot running from his nose.

Mom comes running down the steps to Danny. "Shelby! What on earth's gotten into you?"

I'm panting. "What about him? He . . . he . . ."

"I didn't do anything," Danny cries. "She just started beating me up."

"That's right," Jason says.

"Shelby, get up to the cabin."

"But Mom! You don't understand!" I wipe my mouth

on my sleeve, catching sight of Kirsten still standing on the Dymonds' steps, looking disgusted. "I was just all upset because—"

"Up! Go! Right now!"

I whirl and run up the stone steps to the cabin. I hate them. All of them. Especially my mother. Grown-ups never listen. They never care why somebody does something. They just want everybody to make things nice. As long as everything seems okay on the surface, it doesn't matter what anybody's feeling.

I march into the bathhouse and face myself in the mirror. Good grief! A noise comes out of me, half laugh, half sob. I look like a heavy-metal rocker at the end of a rough gig. Runny makeup, bloody lip and cheek, wild hair . . .

I undo the braids. Then I grab a washcloth and start scrubbing the makeup off.

Mom comes in. She looks tired. She props her elbow on the towel bar and watches me for a minute. Then she sighs. "Why'd you do it, honey?"

Now she wants to know. Now, after she's already made up her mind it's all my fault.

"Does it have anything to do with this new hairdo?"

"What difference does it make?"

"I'm trying to understand you. Can't we talk about it?"

I shake my head. What's the use? Even if I understood myself what Kirsten threatening to drive to Bayport with Tanya has to do with beating up my brother, I'm not going to tell. I don't want to be a tattletale. Telling's one thing if it stops Kirsten from doing something dangerous, another if it's just to get her in trouble.

"I can't believe you started fighting with him for no reason. . . ."

It doesn't make a whole lot of sense, I've got to admit. After all, if I was going to pound somebody, maybe it should have been Tanya. Or Jason. He was the one with the smart remark about me getting boobs. But I'm sure not going to tell my mother *that* . . .

"Excuse me," I say.

She moves aside and I stuff the makeup-streaked towel over the bar.

"You won't tell me anything?"

"No," I say. "You'd never understand in a million years."

Chapter Ten

I'm reading in the window seat two hours later when Aunt Margo breezes in with the groceries. She's stocking up because Uncle Don's coming tomorrow.

"Bad accident at the curve before Bayport," she tells Mom. "At first I just thought, boy, traffic's getting as bad here as everywhere else. Then I saw the ambulance."

I jump up and run into the kitchen. "What color was the car?"

She ignores my question. "Hey, kiddo, where'd you get that scrape?"

"The car, Aunt Margo. Just tell me about the car."

Margo frowns. "What car?"

"The car in the accident."

Mom's giving me a funny look. "Shelby, what's the matter?"

"I just want to know what kind of car it was, okay?"

Mom and Margo glance at each other.

"Well," Margo says, "the one in the ditch was a beige station wagon."

"Oh." I let out a sigh.

"I think they'd already towed the other one away. You

know how it is around here—you can get a tow truck faster than an ambulance."

I hurry to the window. No cars at the house on the point. I dash down to the beach where Kirsten's sunbathing.

"Kirsten! There's been a car accident." I'm breathing hard now. "By Bayport."

"What?" She gets up.

"I think maybe it was Tanya."

"Oh, no." She heads for the path. "Are you sure?"

"No, it's just that her car's not there, and shouldn't she be back by now?"

"Oh, God," Kirsten mutters.

I'm so glad I kept Kirsten from going. Even if they hated me for it. This proves it. This shows you have to stick to what you believe. . . .

But then, just as we reach the Dymonds' steps, Tanya roars up the gravel drive.

Kirsten crosses her arms over her chest, slowly turns, and glares at me.

I shrink. "Well, I thought . . ."

"You thought. Maybe that's your problem. You think too much."

Tanya sees us on her steps. Kirsten starts to raise her hand like she can't decide whether to risk waving or not.

Tanya slams the car door, tosses her hair, and marches into the house.

Kirsten flushes red. She pushes past me and heads back to the beach. "Do me a favor, okay? Just leave me alone."

Someday I'll Laugh About This

* * *

The next morning I lock myself in the bathhouse with Kirsten's magazines. I study the skin-care articles. I study my face in the mirror. A ton of makeup isn't the answer. That's clear. But maybe I could learn to use just a little bit. And Mom's probably right about washing better. The articles say that too. I have to start with the basics . . . good grooming and all that. So I wash my face real thoroughly.

Yuck, these blackheads! I start popping them. Pretty soon my face is a blotchy mess.

A knock on the door. "Shelby?" It's Mom. "What are you doing in there, honey?"

"Nothing." I stuff the magazines under the clothes hamper.

"How about opening up, then? I need the suntan lotion."

I open the door, hoping to slink past her.

"Shelby! *Now* what? Let me see your face."

I hang my head, try to turn away.

"You've been poking at it, haven't you?" She holds my chin, tilting my face to the light. "Honey, that'll just make it worse."

"Well, *you* do it!" I yank away. "You started it, always grabbing me—" I turn, run down the stone steps to the old road, down to the beach, and flop on the blanket we left there. Why can't everyone get off my case? First they nag me for not caring how I look, then they pick on me for trying.

For some reason, lying there, I start thinking about this

program we had in fifth grade for all the girls and our mothers. The school nurse showed a movie about getting your period. I thought it sounded ridiculous, so afterward, when she asked if there were any questions about menstruating, my hand went right up. I go, "Do I have to?" Everybody laughed. Everybody but me, that is. I burst into tears. Not just because I was embarrassed, although that was part of it. Mostly I cried because I hated the idea of not having any choice.

No, there's no choice about growing up—you have to, that's all. I can't keep on being this tomboy who rolls around in ditches pounding her little brother. I guess it's like trees. Unless you die, you've got to grow.

Simple, right? But kind of hard to swallow.

After a while I flip to my back. The sun's good for oily skin, I know that. I've already been in the sun some; now I'm determined to burn these zits off, fry them to smithereens. Every once in a while I remember all over again: Uncle Jack is coming tomorrow! I shut my eyes tight against the light, letting the rhythm of the breakers lull me. I'll look better by then, I promise myself. I *have* to.

"Shelby, will you read to me?"

"Later, Brandon. I'm busy now."

"You don't *look* busy."

Oh, but I am. *It takes pain to be beautiful.* I'm the picture of single-minded determination. And the omens are good. No fog rolls in to ruin my plan. I don't move at all except to rotate my face, following the sun. . . .

* * *

Someday I'll Laugh About This

I wake to find a huge eye staring at me from a black box. I yelp and jump up.

"Uncle Don! That's not funny!" Everyone else is standing around me laughing. I back away and cock my head. "What is that thing?"

"My new toy. A video camera."

"Well, don't take any pictures of me."

"It's taking pictures all the time."

"No!" I put my hands over my face, then peek through my fingers. "When did you get here, anyway?"

"Just now." Uncle Don lowers the camera.

"Looks like you've been working out," Daddy says to him.

Uncle Don grins. "Club membership came with the new job."

Margo play-punches his flat stomach. "Not bad, huh?"

"Brandon, old buddy," he says. "Ready to go after those fish?"

"Yeah!" Brandon jumps up and down. "And Dad? Guess what? Uncle Steve already took me once and I learned some really great techniques!"

"Okay, go get your stuff together."

"Brandon, wait!" Margo yells after him. He's already halfway up the path. "Don't forget your toys."

"When I get back!"

Uncle Don pats his camera like it's a favorite pet. "We'll get the whole thing on film." He turns to Daddy. "I'll show you how, Steve. There's nothing to it. Won't this be great, being able to relive all our memories?"

* * *

105

When they come home from fishing a couple hours later, though, it doesn't sound like the trip was anything they'd want to relive.

Brandon's in tears.

"I hooked a big fish," he wails, "and Dad grabbed the pole away from me!"

"Don!" Margo says. "You didn't!"

"Come on, Margo. I was afraid he'd lose it."

"You didn't even let me try!"

Uncle Don rumples Brandon's hair. "I'm sorry, buddy. I really blew it, didn't I?"

"At any rate," Dad says, "I got the whole thing on video."

"Yeah, uh, I was wondering about that." Uncle Don peels out of his fishing vest. "I've got to figure out how to edit those things. Some of my language was . . . well, not exactly G-rated."

"Uncle Don!" I say. "You were swearing at Brandon?"

"Of course not! I was swearing at the fish." Then he adds quietly, "When he got away."

Mom and Margo groan, then Mom says, "Well, let's start cracking the crab. The kids are getting hungry."

"You got crab?" Dad says. "Great. We were afraid you were counting on our fish."

"Ha!" Mom's look says it all. She *never* counts on them catching dinner.

"Party! Party!" Aunt Margo sings, sashaying around with a little plate of crackers and cheese like she's trying real hard to change the mood.

Someday I'll Laugh About This

Daddy starts panning the room with the video camera. He's nuts about that thing. He aims it at me.

"Daddy, I told you! I don't want to be on film."

"Oh, come on, honey." He never takes his eye from the viewfinder. "Wouldn't you like to watch yourself on TV?"

"Are you kidding?" I head for the stairs to escape. "I don't even like looking in a mirror."

He follows me. "But Shelby, this is a special time in your life. You're not always going to be twelve. I'd like to be able to remember it."

"Turn that off."

Finally he does.

"Daddy," I whisper, "I don't want my picture taken. Not now. I'm ugly."

"Oh, nuts. You're as cute as they come."

Right. I bet every dad in the world thinks his own daughter's cute.

"Why don't you go find Danny and do him some more?" I've watched my brother in action. He doesn't get all self-conscious when he sees the camera aimed at him. He just acts silly, does stuff that's cute at ten but not at twelve. "Or do her." I point at Kirsten. "She likes it."

Daddy aims the camera at Kirsten, who goes on with her manicuring like she's not noticing. That's a laugh. You don't go around trying out weird makeup, sticking glitter on your cheeks and stuff, unless you want people looking at you, right? She turns her head to a more flattering angle.

I plop down, pick up one of her magazines, and hide

107

behind it. She hasn't spoken to me since the big blowup about Tanya driving to Bayport. Even last night in bed. And today it's Pout City, all day long. She's like a little puppy, licking her wounded pride. Oh, boo hoo. The wonderful Tanya called her a kiddie for not going. The wonderful Tanya turned up her nose at us when she came home.

I thumb through the magazine, stopping at a picture of a beautiful girl. Her hair floats around her head, all full of misty flowers. Her cheeks are so clean and smooth. I sigh. That's exactly how I want to look. I read every word of that ad. It's for some kind of scrubbing stuff, something with a little peach on the tube. Boy, it must really work. Just look at that girl's skin. . . .

The screen door bangs. I jump.

"Fences!" Danny pants. "They're blocking off the old road! Come quick!"

I toss aside the magazine and glare at Kirsten. "*Now* will you believe it?"

Everyone rushes out. Mom and Margo try to fill Uncle Don in on all the road and condo rumors as we go.

On the old road just south of Sea Haven we find a couple of guys unrolling chain link between metal posts they've sunk into the soft orange sandstone.

Tanya's father's watching them. I squint into the setting sun at him, my first close-up look. Next to his white windbreaker, his skin looks even darker than Tanya's. His hair's slicked back. Maybe it's a new style, but there's something old-timey about it too. It reminds me of this picture we have of Great-grampa Jenks as a young man. I have to admit, Max Dymond is sort of handsome. At least if you saw him on the street, you wouldn't automatically think, Oh, there's a bad guy.

"What's going on?" Daddy says.

Tanya's father takes his cigarette out of his mouth and blows smoke. "Well, it's time we did something about this, don't you think?"

"Did something about what?"

"Something about all the traffic cutting through our property."

"*Our* property?" Mom says.

"Well, okay, *my* property." He smiles modestly, like he's a little embarrassed to be caught being so generous. "But I think you'll find you're going to benefit from having this access restricted. Less vandalism, littering, that sort of thing."

"Look, Mr. —?"

"Dymond, Max Dymond. Please. Call me Max." He's so smooth. He sticks out his hand.

Dad doesn't have much choice. He shakes it. I notice he looks short next to Tanya's dad.

"In the first place . . . Max," Dad says, "we've never had any trouble with vandalism."

My pulse picks up. I scrunch my shoulders inside my sweatshirt. People argue on TV all the time, snappy remarks zipping back and forth. But in real life, I've noticed, grown-ups hardly ever argue with people they don't know. When they do, it makes you nervous.

"And then, this is a public road," Dad goes on. "You don't have any right to block it off."

The guys setting up the fence stop and look at Max Dymond like they're wondering if they should continue unrolling the chain link or stop. He jerks his head at them, telling them to keep going.

He turns back to us. Above the collar of his purple polo shirt, the muscles in his neck tighten. He's put his smile back on, but it's not natural-looking.

He clears his throat. "Now, you realize you'll still have access to the beach."

Mom's mouth falls open. The very idea! The nerve of the guy! Even to suggest that after sixty years there was the slightest question about this!

"You're darn right we'll have access," she says, "but that's not the half of it. We've always been able to walk all the way into Perpetua. All the neighbors use this road."

"Oh, come on now. You can't call this a road. A bunch of rutted trails through the bushes?"

"Well, it *was* a road," I blurt out. "People used to drive on it."

"That's right," Mom says. "And legally, I think it still is."

Wow. My heart's thumping. I can't believe I spoke up like that.

Max Dymond looks very uncomfortable now. "No, no. My lawyers have checked all that out." He rotates his shoulders and jerks his neck to the side like he's trying to unkink knotted muscles.

Mom crosses her arms over her chest. "If this had been vacated, we'd have been notified, wouldn't we, since our lot borders it?"

"And what about eminent domain?" Aunt Margo says.

110

"Like we said, everyone's used this for years. You can't just close off a public access."

"Hey, hey," Max Dymond says, holding up his hands. "I don't quite understand where you folks are coming from. I'd say giving up a rutty trail to town is a small price to pay for keeping the public from trampling through here."

"But it's never been a problem," Mom says.

"You wait, it will be." His voice changes. Suddenly he's a grown-up trying to be patient with a stubborn child. "Look, this is really in your best interest. Restrict this access and you know what'll happen to your property values?" He leans toward Mom and jerks his thumb at the sky. "Straight up."

"Big deal," Mom shoots right back. "Higher taxes."

"No, no, don't you get it? Then you sell for a terrific profit! In fact, I'm prepared to make you a very handsome offer on your lot myself." He throws his cigarette on the ground. "I'm going to need all the land I can put together with the way the county's on me about having plenty of parking spaces for my condos."

I suck in my breath. Sea Haven . . . a parking lot?

Mom's eyes narrow. "As far as I can see, Mr. Dymond, you're right about just one thing. You *don't* understand where this family's coming from!"

Chapter Eleven

"Take it easy," Uncle Don says, tossing an empty crab-leg shell into the big bowl in the middle of the table. "All I said was, it'd be interesting to hear the guy's offer."

"I wouldn't care if it was a million dollars," Mom says. "We'd never sell Sea Haven."

"Well, actually," Aunt Margo puts in, "for a million, I reserve the right to think about it. . . ."

"Margo!"

"Come on, Nance. Calm down. You're making it sound like we're hinting at selling one of the kids, for crying out loud!"

"Well, to me, it comes pretty darn close!" Mom pushes up from the table and goes over in front of the fireplace. "Right here," she says, aiming her finger straight down at the braided rug. "It was right on this very spot that Shelby was conceived."

I about choke on a chunk of crab. Does that mean what I think it means? I glance at Kirsten, who blushes and rolls her eyes. My face goes red hot too. That's what it means, all right. Wow. I swallow, staring at the worn threads of the braid rug. I can't picture my parents . . . I shake my head. I don't *want* to. But still, to think that this is the very place in the whole universe where I came into being . . .

"Speaking of Shelby," Dad says. "Did you catch the way she spoke right up to that guy?" He gives me a scrunch-mouthed little smile.

I swear, parents are so hard to understand. Here I'd been halfway expecting to get in trouble for sassing a grown-up, and instead he's proud of me.

"I'm so glad Jack's coming," Mom goes on. "I bet he'd have a fit if anybody so much as put *sell* and *Sea Haven* in the same sentence. This place means a lot to him."

"You know, Don, she's right," Margo says, her voice softening. "Sea Haven means a lot to me too. Think of all the memories . . ."

Uncle Don gazes at Margo over another crab leg. "That summer we were first going together . . ."

Margo sighs. "Our honeymoon . . ."

"The first time we brought Kirsten . . ."

"Ha!" Margo's mushiness is gone, zip. "You took off fishing and left me with colic and diapers!"

"Now, now," Mom says, starting to clear the plates. "Make things nice!"

After the dishes are done, Daddy builds a fire and Margo pours out the wine Uncle Don brought. Kirsten sulks behind a magazine, but at least the grown-ups are in good moods. Now that Uncle Don's here, it seems more like a party, a party that's gotten off to an exciting start with this argument over Max Dymond's fences.

I throw the cushions off the window seat and lift the

hinged lid. It's about time I kept my promise to Mrs. Blake to dig out the old logbooks.

"We've got to find evidence," I tell everyone. "Mrs. Blake's getting a lawyer. We've got to be able to prove people have used the road all those years."

I start from the beginning, 1927, putting a paper marker in the musty-smelling books each time I find a "walked to town on the bluff path" entry. And there are lots. That's the sort of thing Mama Jenks wrote about: "Finished this chore, took that walk. Nice weather, bad weather."

"This doesn't make any sense." I read from the book: " 'Terribly dusty drive over. Road could use some rain.' What does she mean? I've never seen the road dusty."

"It was, though," Mom says. "Until the 1950s, Highway 34 was gravel from the Lincoln County line on."

"You're kidding."

"No, I'm not."

"Did you kids realize," Daddy says, "that it's only been in the last fifty years that there were bridges across the coast rivers? Before that people had to use ferries."

"But fifty years ago is a long time," Kirsten says.

"Not really," Daddy says. "Not compared to how long most other parts of the country have been settled and paved."

I try to imagine what it was like here, completely wild. Then I try to picture it fifty years in the future when I'm almost Gramma B.'s age. It worries me. I hope some of the wildness will be left. I hope the people like Tanya's father won't ruin everything.

Mom brings out hot chocolate for us and I start to feel better. At least right now things are okay. It's cozy, sitting on the window-seat cushions, my face glowy from all those hours in the sun. I sip my chocolate.

"How old was Gramma B. when Grampa Jenks built Sea Haven?" I ask Mom.

"Eleven."

"Hmm." I skim through a few more years. A lot of it's pretty boring. Once in a while there's a clipping about a big storm or a whale that washed up on the beach. One little newspaper article taped to the page tells about a guy who got killed by a driftlog up near Bayport. But mostly Grampa B. wrote about the weather. "Hey, why is there this big gap between 1941 and 1945?"

Daddy looks up from his book about fishing, the funny one he reads every summer at the cabin. "World War II."

Mom pokes at the fire. "Dad always said that with the gas rationing, they just couldn't come over. And then, too, people were nervous about being on the coast. They were always afraid the Japanese might land."

"Gee," I say.

"You know the stone lookout up on Cape Perpetua? That's what it was built for. To watch for enemy ships."

Margo refills the grown-ups' wineglasses. "Your Gramma B. always talks about how wonderful it was when they finally got to come back. That was the war really being over for her, coming back to Sea Haven."

Nobody says anything for a while as the fire pops and hisses.

Then Mom speaks quietly. "It's pretty incredible when

116

you think about it, isn't it? I mean, our family history here is longer than it's been anywhere else. We've all lived in a lot of different houses, and now you guys have even left Oregon, but we've always come back here. How many people have something like that?"

We *are* lucky. I try to memorize each face glowing in the firelight. The boys lying on the floor with their comics, Brandon with his catalog, Kirsten with her magazine. The grown-ups are cuddled on the two sofas. It's all kind of reassuring. Deep down, in spite of our squabbles, everybody here likes everybody else. I think Danny's even forgiven me for pounding him. At least he shared the last Dove Bar with me. If that isn't forgiveness, I don't know what is.

No, what we have, money can't buy. Even if dumb old Max Dymond bought this place for a million dollars, all he'd be getting is a little cottage; he could never take away our good times. That has to do with us being a family, part of something that keeps going on. Then I have a funny thought. Maybe our family's like Brandon's Returnity Belt, protecting us and growing along with us no matter what happens. . . .

I go back to the logs. "Listen to this. 'August 10, 1962. Dance in Perpetua. Fun, but don't imagine we'll try leaving girls alone like that again. They've been told—we don't want to see Bobby Lucas around here again.' " I look up from the book. "It bugs me that they leave out so much. Like who was Bobby Lucas?"

"Oh, Lord," Margo says, kind of dreamy-eyed.

"Bobby Lucas," Mom repeats in the same tone.

117

"Who's that?" Kirsten asks, her first flicker of interest.

"By all means," Uncle Don says, "let's get to the bottom of this."

"Bobby Lucas was a boy I liked one summer," Margo starts out. "He was really cute."

"Not that cute," Mom says. "I think you just liked him because of the song."

"What song?" I ask.

Mom's eyes meet Margo's. They giggle. Then they jump up and start singing.

"I wanna be . . . Bobby's girl
I wanna be . . . Bobby's girl
That's the most . . . important thing to-o me-e . . ."

"Oh, for Pete's sake," Kirsten mutters, embarrassed to death.

But Mom and Margo don't give a hoot. They mug their way through all the verses, eyes half closed. Teens in love.

Danny and Jason trade do-you-believe-this looks as Mom and Margo shake their hair, hunch up their shoulders, bebop around the room.

But Brandon loves it—grown-ups going crazy—and when they jump up on Gramma B.'s mosaic table for a finale, he joins them, singing into a Transformer for a mike.

Then, exhausted, Mom and Margo flop on the sofa and lay there flushed and panting.

"Do you know these chicks?" Uncle Don says to Daddy.

"I didn't bring 'em. I thought *you* did."

"If you guys are going to act like such geeks," Kirsten says, "how about closing the curtains? Don't you realize the Dymonds' place has a perfect view of this window?"

"No! Really?" Mom jumps up and gives a big howdy wave to the house on the point, convulsing Margo in giggles.

Disgusted, Kirsten marches over and yanks the curtains closed.

"Oh, gee, Margo," Mom says. "It must be tough to be young and have to act so serious all the time."

"Yeah . . ." Margo's head rests on the sofa back. Without lifting it, she turns to Mom. "But, really, it's not true about the song being the reason I liked him. I had a much more *mature* reason." She lays her hand over her heart. "I was deeply, passionately in love with Bobby Lucas because . . ."

"Because . . . ?"

"Because he was the only boy we'd ever met here!"

Mom clobbers her with a patchwork pillow.

Brandon takes the cue. He lets one fly at Daddy, and the fight's on. Even Kirsten winds up swinging a pillow. The stuffing poofs out the torn corner with every whap and sticks in her hair.

"Hey wait," I holler, ducking an old needlepoint number Jason lobs my way. "You still haven't told us why this kid wasn't supposed to come around."

By this time everybody's got red faces and messy hair. We all start marching around chanting, "Bobby Lucas! Bobby Lucas!"

119

"Well," Mom begins as we sprawl on the floor to listen, "Mom and Dad went to that dance she mentions and left us in charge of Jack. After we had him in bed, Bobby came over. Of course, we weren't supposed to have boys here while they were gone—same rule as at home." She takes a sip of wine. "And Margo knew that perfectly well."

"So did you," Margo points out.

"Yes, but you were older. You were in charge."

"All right, all right . . ."

"Anyway," Mom goes on cheerfully, "Margo's hero offers to help us jazz up the fire, since we'd kind of let it die down, see? So he gets the can of lawn mower gas from the shed—"

"Oh, no—"

"And throws some on the fire!"

"Wow," Danny says. "Bad news. You're never supposed to do that."

"That's right," Mom says. "And I'll never forget how the flames roared up. It was—it was—"

"Awesome," Jason finishes for her.

"Exactly." Mom exhales like she just now lived through the near tragedy of it. "We were so lucky. We could have burned the whole place down."

All eyes turn toward the charred spot on the ceiling beam above the hearth. I'm trying to imagine how the flames must have whooshed up that night.

"But Mom," Kirsten says, "you always told us you didn't know how that burned place got there."

"Did I? Well, I guess I wasn't too proud of the story."

Someday I'll Laugh About This

"So, did you get in trouble?" Jason asks.

Mom and Aunt Margo look at each other.

"Aunt Nancy tattled," Margo says.

"Come on, they would have seen the beam, anyway."

"But the way you couldn't *wait* to tell on me for having Bobby over . . ."

"Well . . ." Mom sighs. "I guess I was jealous."

"I don't believe it!" Margo turns to the rest of us. "It's only taken her twenty-five years to admit that!"

I study my mom's face in the firelight. Maybe she does understand certain things. Maybe this is what she meant by that saying, The more things change, the more they stay the same.

"So what did they do to you?" I ask. "Gramma and Grampa B., I mean."

"Oh, your mom wasn't punished at all," Margo says. "She was just the innocent little sister."

"I was too punished," Mom says. "My punishment was that Mom never told me what *your* punishment was. She wasn't about to let me have the satisfaction."

"Too bad."

"So what *did* she do to you?"

Margo smiles sweetly. "I'll never tell."

"Oh, you!" Mom halfheartedly swings a pillow at Margo, then hugs it tightly to herself. "As I recall, we didn't speak to each other for the rest of the vacation. In fact, I remember worrying that you'd never speak to me again. You were so *mad*!"

I glance at Kirsten. Funny thing—she's looking at me too. Suddenly I get this idea. Maybe someday Kirsten and I will be sitting here with families of our own, drinking a little wine, acting silly, and telling our kids stories about the terrible fights we had all those years ago.

Maybe we'll even be laughing about it.

Chapter Twelve

Now this is the best omen of all!

Kirsten must have left it here in the shower stall, a tube of the very same stuff I saw in the magazine. It's got that little peach right on it! I seize the tube. I'll show no mercy. I'll scrub my face so hard, no blackhead can possibly survive.

I squirt out a big glob of the grainy stuff and rub it around my face with a washcloth. I scrub and scrub, everywhere except where my cheek is scraped. It feels like sandpaper, but if determination alone can make me beautiful, I've got it made! Then I give my hair a good shampooing. Optimism washes over me like hot water. Uncle Jack's coming tomorrow and I'm going to look just fine.

I step out, swipe a clean streak across the steamy mirror, and peer at myself. Ah! Rosy and smooth . . .

I comb every last snarl out of my hair. Then I practice wistful expressions as I blow it dry. I make it fan out from my head and pretend it's twined with misty blossoms like the girl in the magazine. . . .

* * *

Linda Crew

A huge black wave is coming at me, churning across the beach. Run, *run*! But my legs keep sinking into the sand. The roar gets louder as I reach the slippery path. I don't dare look back. I have to get to the cabin, get home where I'll be safe. I can't breathe, can't get out a yell for help.

But look! Flames, leaping from the cabin! I have to get inside and find Uncle Jack. Or Brandon. *Somebody*. My face is hot, burning. . . .

I lurch up, awake. Ah! I let out a big sigh. I'm tucked into my bed under the eaves at Sea Haven. The ocean is just a soft, lulling rumble out beyond the wide sand beach. The only fire is the one that would barely be glowing by now, down in the big stone fireplace.

"Whassa matter?" Kirsten mumbles.

"Bad dream."

"Well, could you please stop thrashing around?" She pulls her pillow over her head.

"Sorry." But wait a minute . . . good grief! "Kirsten! Kirsten, wake up." I put my palms to my cheeks. That stinging. Something's wrong. I mean, *really* wrong. I wave my arms for the dangling light bulb string and yank it.

"Owwww. Turn that off!"

"Kirsten, look at my face for me. It's on fire."

Bleary-eyed, Kirsten blinks at me. "You're probably sunburned." She pulls the light off. "Now go back to sleep."

I stare into the darkness. I touch my face. It feels . . . well, *raw*. Should I sneak down and check it out in the mirror? No, somebody'd be sure to wake up. The last

124

thing I need is a lot of questions. Is it possible this is the pain it takes to make you beautiful?

I sleep fitfully, and at first light I wake to the sound of Daddy and Uncle Don backing the car out to go fishing. The burning in my face is gone. Good. It's going to be okay. Relieved, I touch my chin. Oh, no! I bolt upright. What's *that*? I hurry my fingers over my face. It's hard, crusty. I fling back the covers and dash downstairs. At the bathhouse, I push open the door and run to the mirror.

I stare. A leathery crust circles my mouth, a big brown clown smile. A cry chokes out of me. I stagger back inside through the kitchen to the main room, half crazy. I've ruined my face. Today of all days. The day Uncle Jack is coming!

Kirsten's magazines are neatly stacked on the big round table. Those dumb things! They lie! They trick you into believing you can be pretty if you use that junk . . . and then *this* happens! They ought to be against the law! I wish I'd never seen them! I snatch one up and rip at the pages, hurling wads into the fireplace. Rip! Got that one right across her dopey white smile. Rip! Take that, you witch! Rip and wad, rip and wad . . . I guess I'm louder about all this than I realize. People are waking up.

"What on earth . . . ?" comes from the bedroom. "What's happening?"

I collapse on the sofa and pull a cushion over my head.

"Hey, people are trying to sleep." Mom comes out in her flannel nightgown.

Danny and Kirsten come down the stairs.

125

"Shelby," Mom says, "you know better than to—honey, what's wrong? Why are you hiding your face?"

"No, don't look!" My voice is muffled. "I don't want anyone to see!"

"Come on now." Mom sits on the edge of the couch and we do a little tug-of-war with the pillow. She's not mean about it but she's determined. Finally she wins.

"My God. What happened?"

"Wow!" Danny says. "Grody to the max!"

"Shut up!" I croak. "Just shut up!"

Brandon creeps in behind Jason. I can tell just how awful I look by the size of his eyes. "She must have gotten zapped by an alien ray gun," he says.

Mom seems completely baffled. "Could the sun do this?"

"I guess," I say. "I stayed out a long time. And I . . . maybe I washed my face too hard."

"Oh, God," Kirsten says. "How totally dumb."

Mom's head snaps around. "Kirsten!"

"Well really, Aunt Nancy, she—hey, wait a minute. Look what she did to my magazines!" She picks up the tatters, glares at me, then throws them back on the table. "You're in for it now." She makes for her parents' room. "Mo-om!"

I bolt past them all, scramble up the stairs, and fling myself on the bed. Mom's right behind me.

"Leave me alone!"

But Mom doesn't leave. She just sits there while I cry it out.

"Oh, Mom, I . . . I wanted to be . . . when I found out Uncle Jack was coming, I just wanted . . ."

"I know, I know," Mom says, rocking me in her warm, flannelly arms. After a while she pulls on the light and turns my face to it. "Oh, honey . . ." She winces like she hurts too. "It looks like you just took the top layer of skin right off. That's why it scabbed over. But I don't think it'll scar."

"Scar!" A fresh burst of tears. I haven't even thought of that. It's bad enough having it like this for one day, when it's the one day Uncle Jack is coming.

"Now, honey . . ."

"By the time he got here I wanted to be different. I'm tired of being a fat, dopey little girl."

"You're not a fat, dopey little girl."

"I *feel* like it, though, and I wanted to *change*."

"You'll change soon enough without rushing it. Don't you know you're fine just the way you are?"

"Oh, sure. I'm just fine with a monster face."

"I don't mean your face. I mean you. Your face'll heal up pretty soon."

"Won't make any difference. Kirsten'll still be prettier than me." I stick my chin out. "And don't try telling me she isn't."

"I'm not going to tell you that."

I blink. "You're not?"

"You wouldn't believe me, would you?"

"No." I sniff. "But I thought you'd at least be rooting for your own kid."

"Shelby, I *do* root for you. Don't you know that?"

127

"But I just hate it, her being prettier and older and everything."

"I know," Mom says. "And nothing I can say's going to change that." She looks out the little window toward the beach. "You know something?" She turns back to me. "Just between you and me, I wish I could have shredded those magazines with you."

"Mom!"

"Well, it makes me mad too. Why do we have to keep comparing ourselves to these models? Why can't we be satisfied to be regular, decent-looking people? Sure, it's fine to look your best, but after a point . . . well, frankly, I don't want to have to do sixty-five sit-ups a day, and I don't care what Margo says!"

I stop crying and look at her. She's not just mad for me. She's mad for herself too.

"But Mom," I say, "if you don't look like that, you won't get a boyfriend. You'll never get married."

"Oh, phooey! I got your dad, didn't I? I got you kids. You don't have to be a beauty queen to find somebody to love. And anyway, there's a lot more to life than boyfriends and finding a mate—interesting careers, traveling . . ."

"But those magazine pictures . . . you know the one where her hair's all floating out with flowers?"

"Yes, yes, it's beautiful, I know. But it's just a photograph. It's not real life. Would you want to walk down the halls of Western View with your hair three feet in the air and a garden growing out of it?"

Okay, she gets a smile out of me.

"But it's real in those pictures where the girls are on the beach with all the boys. . . ."

"Are you kidding? Those models are probably freezing their rears off because they're taking those pictures in the dead of winter. They're not really having a picnic, they're just standing around acting happy for a camera. But you—you really *are* at the beach."

"Not with boys."

Mom laughs. "Because there *aren't* any boys here. You know that. Now look, Shelby, I'm sure if you want boyfriends, you'll have boyfriends. But you've got to understand something—the world's not divided into happy women who have husbands and miserable women who don't. Believe me, I know some pretty unhappy women who don't feel one bit lucky that they have husbands."

"But you're happy with Dad, right?"

"Of course! I'm just trying to point out that happiness doesn't have to depend on some guy. Your happiness is going to depend on you."

I give her a doubtful look. "Yeah?"

"And as far as looking like a model, you've got something much better going for you."

"Huh. Like what?"

"You're smart. Shelby, you've got a mind like a steel trap."

"Oh, puleeze! You call this smart? Scrubbing my skin off? And even if I was smart, what's the use of it?"

"Trust me, honey. You're not always going to feel this way. This is a hard time for you. You're just at an awkward stage."

129

"No kidding." I let out a long sigh. "I wish I could run away or something. I wish they had a place you could go when you got this way. Camp Awkward Stage, they could call it, where the people have to accept you and take care of you until you're through it."

"There is a place like that," Mom says, putting her arms around me again. "It's called home. It's called Sea Haven. And the people are your family."

Chapter Thirteen

I'm sprawled facedown on the beach blanket. I have a book, but who wants to read? Suddenly I get the feeling I'm not alone. I open my eyes. Mrs. Blake's green rubber boots. She eases herself onto a huge log and I have to explain all over again how I wrecked my face and got this big brown scab.

"Isn't that the stupidest thing you ever heard of?" I ask her when I'm done.

She starts laughing—just a little simper at first, then it grows into a chuckle. She has to wipe her eyes.

"Well really," I say, "I don't think it's one bit funny."

"I know, I know," she says. "Can't help it, though. You brought to mind an old memory, something I'll bet I haven't thought of in sixty years."

"Yeah? What's that?" She's got me curious now. What could be so funny that an old lady would start laughing herself to tears right out of the blue?

"Well, there was this girl my friend and I admired. Something of a hussy, but we were jealous of her looks. I guess she knew how we felt and kind of enjoyed leading us on. So one day she tells us she'll let us in on her beauty secret. Do you know what it was?"

I shake my head.

Mrs. Blake leans toward me and whispers so Brandon can't hear. "She told us to wash our faces in our own pee!"

"You're kidding."

"And we did it! Oh, she had a laugh on us, all right."

"Wow." I make a face. "I can't believe you did that."

"Believe it, girl."

Boy, that really is gross.

"Okay," I say, "so I'm not the first person to do something dumb. This is still the worst thing that's ever happened to me. Because today's the day my uncle Jack's coming."

"Is that so? Say, I always look forward to seeing that boy. What a charmer. Sends me a Christmas card every year, regular as rain."

"He does?" Uncle Jack isn't known for being regular about anything.

"Well, I've fed him a cookie or two over the years, you know."

Uncle Jack gobbling cookies. Yeah, I can see it. Some grown-ups are easier to picture as kids than others.

"I've sat right here and watched him diggin' away in the sand just like this little fella here," Mrs. Blake says, nodding at Brandon. She starts in on how Jack used to play with her grandson.

I'm sorry, but at the moment this doesn't interest me much. Usually I like stories about old times, but sometimes "right now" just kind of blots out everything else. Especially when "right now" is so horrible.

132

Someday I'll Laugh About This

"I hate to have Uncle Jack see me like this," I say when she's done. "He's bringing his fiancée."

"Somebody finally snagged him, hm?"

"Guess so." I run my fingers over my crusty cheek. "My mom says being smart is better than being pretty. Do you think that's true?"

"Well," Mrs. Blake says, "smart lasts longer. The peak of pretty lasts about five or ten years—not much in a good long life like mine." She thinks a moment. "Being smart, though—well, it's like being pretty, isn't it? Maybe you are, maybe you aren't. It's just something you're given. What counts ought to be where you take it from there."

This sort of throws me. At school, as far as the teachers are concerned, smart is best. I thought I could at least rely on that.

"You see, being smart doesn't make you a good person," Mrs. Blake goes on. "Not to my mind. Look at this Max Dymond. He's smart. He's real smart. But look what he's doing with it. Do you know I counted six sets of fences on the old road trail this morning? And that's just before I gave up trying to get through. Devil of a time. Looks like Dymond's got a few other landowners going along with him—the motel and whoever owns the vacant parcels by Dead Man's Gulch."

"Great," I say. "Just great." I stare out at the ocean for a while. "But what you were saying before, about being pretty or smart? Well, if being pretty's no good, and neither is being smart, what *is* good?"

"Don't misunderstand me, girl. Those things are fine.

But what's better is something harder to hang a name on." She jabs her stick into the sand, then looks up to watch Brandon digging. "Call it heart."

"Heart?"

Mrs. Blake nods. "Being a person who cares about things. Things beyond herself."

I shiver. Right now I don't feel like a person with any of these qualities.

"Wasn't there some old song about that?" Mrs. Blake says. "Sure. Something about 'it's fine to be a genius, of course, but keep the cart before the horse.' " She sings in a cracked voice, " 'You gotta have heart . . .' "

I try to smile, but her singing is embarrassing.

"I think brave is best," Brandon says. "Brave is something you have to try to be."

"Now there's a thought," Mrs. Blake says.

Well, people can talk all they want about being brave and smart and caring about other people, but what good does it do if the rest of the world agrees that beautiful is best? Beautiful is what makes people like you, right? And isn't that what everybody wants? For other people to like them? I guess in the end that's what I really want. . . .

The morning clouds aren't lifting today. Everything is shades of gray and white and misty blue—except for Kirsten, sitting by herself down the beach in her pink-and-purple jams. She looks like the spot of color the watercolor artists always add to their beach pictures.

Mom and Margo haven't even been down yet. Maybe they're still up at the cabin slamming dishes around, arguing about raising kids. I got a real earful through the heating grate after I stopped crying and Mom went downstairs. Margo thought I ought to be punished for wrecking the magazines, but Mom told her I was miserable enough.

Then, just when Margo gets going on the virtues of letting kids suffer the consequences of their own actions, Brandon bursts in crying that the Star Wars figures he left on the beach yesterday were swept out by the tide. Right away Margo promises him new ones, and Mom says, "Great, Margo. That's teaching him."

About this time Daddy and Uncle Don come home arguing about why they didn't catch any blueback. Uncle Don always wants to use big shiny lures, but Daddy thinks they're not fair to the fish. Somehow this works into a four-way fight about where Jack and Kate will sleep. Sleeping bags on the sofas have always been the rule for the last to arrive, but now Margo thinks a double bed ought to be vacated for them since they're engaged. Personally I think she just wants to be the one to make points with Jack.

"They can have a double bed when they're married," Dad says. "In the meantime it's a lousy example for the kids."

"But sleeping bags won't fool anybody," Uncle Don says.

"Fooling people isn't the point," Mom says. "The point is, Sea Haven still belongs to Mom and Dad, and you know they wouldn't approve . . ."

I kick at the sand and sigh. People bickering, people not speaking to each other, people calling people monster face. . . . If this is still going on when Gramma and Grampa B. come next weekend . . . well, we aren't exactly making things nice, are we? What happened to all those good feelings from last night, anyway?

They're gone, that's what, and we'll never get them back. Not exactly in the same way. It's a lot more complicated than just going, "Hey, I know! I'll get out the logbooks. Mom and Margo, you start acting silly and . . ."

No, you can't repeat a good time. I first found that out back when Brandon begged us for a rerun on what we always called the Night of the Pig Noses—a wild evening of grunting up and down the stairs with our noses Scotch-taped pig-style up to our foreheads. Brandon hated that he'd missed out, being a baby, so he bugged us until finally we gave in and tried it again. The minute I put the tape on my nose, though, I knew it wouldn't be the same. Maybe by then we were too old. We felt silly.

Now I see that you can't even do the same thing the very next day in the same place with the same people and expect it to turn out right. It's like we're all in motion, caught up in our own changes. No choice but to keep moving on to something new.

I sift dry sand between my fingers. Tiny crystals, black, amber and clear. Once they were huge rocks, but the ocean ground them up. If the ocean can grind rocks, why can't it grind plastic? And as long as I'm brooding, why do all the good things—friends, family, favorite places—have to change, but the bad things, like six-pack rings, last four hundred years? Sometimes it just seems like . . . well, like life isn't set up right.

Someday I'll Laugh About This

"Here she comes," Mrs. Blake says now. "That odd-looking one. The Dymond girl."

"Wonderful."

"Those blank eyes of hers." Mrs. Blake shudders. "I can't abide people who look right through you like you're not there." She stands up in three separate jerks. "Better go bake some cookies." She gives me a little poke with her stick. "Cheer up, girl. You're going to be fine."

Cheer up? Oh, sure. I bury my face in the blanket.

"I wonder," Brandon says, stopping his shoveling for a moment. "When my Luke Skywalker was standing on top of my fort, and that wave came and knocked him off, do you think he remembered to go *aaaahhhhhhh*?"

"He better have," I mumble into the blanket, "after all the practice he's had."

I keep my face down as Tanya passes without speaking. Is she going to snub Kirsten too?

I can't resist checking.

No, she isn't. She and Kirsten are talking, hands in their sweatshirt pockets, bare feet scuffing at the sand. Looks like Tanya's forgiven Kirsten for chickening out on the drive to Bayport. And I guess Kirsten doesn't give a hoot that it's this girl's father who's blocking our road with fences and threatening to ruin the place. I watch them amble up the beach together. Traitorous, that's what it is.

I try to go back to reading my book, but after a while I glance up again. Now they're standing on this big log that must have rolled in last night. It's not a downed tree—no roots or branches. It must have come from a mill up one of the rivers—probably broke loose from a raft of logs.

Hey, wait a minute. The waves are coming up around it. I let out a long, disgusted sigh. I suppose I ought to remind them how dangerous that is . . . as if Kirsten hasn't heard this warning a thousand times. But she'd probably just tell me to butt out, and Tanya'd laugh at my scabby face. And if I run up and tell, they'll call me a tattletale again.

No, forget it.

I prop my chin in my hands and watch Tanya testing her balance, stepping those long brown legs of hers up and down the length of the log. She's wearing orange and green jams, adding another spot of color to the gray picture. The wind wraps her white-blond hair around her face, and she pulls it away, saying something to Kirsten at the other end of the log. Then both of them turn and look in my direction.

I turn away real fast. They're talking about me. I can tell.

"Hey, look at those guys," Brandon says. "I thought we weren't supposed to do that."

"You're right. We're not."

Darn, it does look like fun, though, trying to stay balanced as the log rocks a little with an incoming wave. Watch. They'll have a good time and get away with it, just like Tanya gets away with everything. Meanwhile I have to be this goody-goody and follow all the grown-ups' rules.

And what have I ever gotten for taking grown-ups' advice? Well, I got humiliated at a boy-girl party. And what about the fire drill last winter? A hundred times Mrs. Caldwell's told us to get out fast when the fire alarm goes off. "Don't wait for anything," she says. So the bell rings after PE one day and I'm in the shower. Stupid, do-what-I'm-told me, I grab a towel and head for the door. Everyone else goes, "Hey, it's just a drill." They put on their clothes and then come out to make fun of me, the only one nearly naked and shivering in the cold. But maybe Mrs. Caldwell, at least, is pleased I take her so seriously? No way. She's annoyed at *me* because now she's got all these howling boys on her hands.

No, I've had it. Being a goody-goody doesn't pay.

I glance up at the cabin. Why don't Margo and the others come to the window and see what's happening? Hustle down here and tell Kirsten to get off?

A few minutes later I'm sneaking another peek at Tanya and Kirsten.

Brandon!

He's out on the log with them. He holds up his stick sword against the gray sky. I can barely hear him over the ocean's roar, but I know what he's yelling. "I . . . have . . . the power!"

Oh, brother. If anything happened to that kid . . . I put down my book, get up, and kick down the beach toward the log. My heart's thudding. They're going to hate me even more for this.

I take a deep breath. "You guys really better get off."

"Oh, go on," Kirsten says. "I've had it with you being such a drag."

139

Linda Crew

"Hey," Tanya says, "you *did* screw up your face."

I ignore her. "Kirsten, you *know* you're not supposed to play on drift logs."

"Come on, this thing's not going anywhere."

She's got a point. The waves have sucked out again and the log's just sitting there on the wet sand. It looks like cedar, about a foot and a half in diameter. I'm standing close enough to see the little live sea creatures on it poking out from their shells.

I almost wish the log would roll just enough to give Kirsten a healthy scare. But it doesn't. The next wave laps up, barely rocking it. Tanya and Kirsten are standing close together now at the far end, giving me ugly looks. Brandon's balanced at the end near me.

Oh well, since I'm already the complete loser in this summer's Sea Haven popularity contest, I might as well go all the way.

"Come on, Brandon." I throw an arm around his waist and haul him off the log.

"Lemme go! Lemme go!" He's kicking and screaming.

"No, Brandon, now stop it. You wanna wind up flat as a pancake?" Even I know I'm exaggerating. I probably *am* just a stupid party pooper.

And then, before I've even let him go, a white wave hits the log. Kirsten jumps forward, Tanya falls back.

Brandon stops struggling and clings to me as the cold wave surges against my calves, pulls sand from under my feet. I stagger with him as the water keeps coming. Finally the forward rush stops and I realize Kirsten's screaming.

140

Someday I'll Laugh About This

"It got her!" Brandon hollers. "The log got her!"

He means Tanya. She's down by the log and she's not jumping up.

My ears roar. The wave's pulling back out. I hold Brandon steady until he can stand on his own, then I aim him toward the dry sand. He takes off. I turn and splash back toward Tanya.

The log rolled. That's what keeps going through my head: The log actually rolled. Just like they always warn us. My heart's about to gag me when I get to Tanya. Her leg's bent back, pinned under the log.

"Get it off!" she's moaning. "Get it off!"

"Kirsten! Get ready to pull her."

"What?"

"You've got to pull her away when I lift the log."

Kirsten's ready to freak out. "But . . . but . . ."

"Do what I say." This rush of energy goes through me. I don't think about the log being too heavy. I think how the next big wave's going to roll it right over her. And *that* I'm not about to stand here and watch.

Kirsten wraps her arms under Tanya's armpits. I wedge my hands between the log and the sand and lift.

"Now," I grunt.

Kirsten jerks her back and I drop the log. Tanya's leg looks pretty banged up. I yell for Brandon to go for help, but he's already halfway to the cabin. Okay, I think. Chalk one up for smart.

Together Kirsten and I help Tanya limp up to the dry sand. Suddenly my knees turn so rubbery, I have to sit down. Bad case of the close-call shakes, I guess. Shoot, I

Linda Crew

came so close to leaving Brandon on the log. Maybe I'd almost come to believe his theory myself: Nothing bad has happened so far, nothing bad ever *can* happen. But it's not true. One blink and you could be Pancake City.

A few neighbors come down out of their cabins. They must have been watching the whole thing through their front windows. *Now* they come, I think. Thanks a lot. I stand up. My legs still feel strange. I go back for the army blanket to put over Tanya.

"God, it really hurts," Tanya moans. "I must've cracked the bone."

Mom, Dad, Don, and Margo come scurrying down the path behind Brandon. Dad takes a look at Tanya's leg and heads up to get her father.

"What on earth were you girls thinking?" Mom demands, covering Tanya with the blanket again. "Why didn't you tell her it was dangerous?"

Kirsten gets this sick look and drops her head between her knees.

"Shelby did," Brandon says. "But Kirsten was out there doing it too! She even let *me* do it!"

Margo's head snaps up. "Kirsten!"

Kirsten starts to sniff.

"You mean, you kids were on the log when it rolled?" Margo looks from one to the other.

"Not me," Brandon says. "Shelby pulled me off."

"But you were, Kirsten?"

Kirsten nods without lifting her head.

"She just got lucky and fell forward," I explain.

142

"Oh, my God," Margo says. "How many times have we told you guys . . ."

Poor Margo. She's about ready to fall apart. It gets me when grown-ups start to lose it like this.

"Come on, Aunt Margo." I run my wet sleeve under my nose. "Don't cry."

"I'm not," she says, and then she bursts into tears.

Mom puts her arm around my shoulders and gives me a squeeze.

Chapter Fourteen

"Think she'd better have an X ray?" Dad asks Max Dymond, who's stooping over Tanya now.

"Looks like it. Where'd you say the closest place was?"

"Newport."

Mr. Dymond sighs. "Honestly, sweetheart, of all the dumb things to do . . ."

"*Daddy.* I'm hurt."

"Yeah, okay. Sorry, babe. We'll save the lectures for later."

"She probably didn't understand how dangerous it is," Mom says. "Lots of times people from out of state don't."

"Hey, I'd love to give her the benefit of the doubt," he says, "but I've warned her about this myself. And it's on all those green signs." He shakes his head and looks at Tanya. "This isn't going to be much fun explaining to your mother, is it? Especially if you wind up in a cast."

Actually, it's a miracle something worse than a banged-up leg hasn't happened sooner, the way Tanya does everything but send out engraved invitations: "Trouble, you are cordially invited . . ."

Her father scoops her up in his arms. She lets her wet

blond head rest against his chest. Funny, even though her leg hurts, she looks . . . well, content.

I glance at Kirsten to see if she's picking up on this, but she's got the heel of her hand pressed to her eye and isn't focusing on much of anything.

Watching Tanya put her arms around her father's neck, I think I'm starting to get it. She doesn't hate her father at all. She loves him. Maybe what she's been trying to say all along is actually this: "Daddy, you are cordially invited to notice that trouble is readily available and I'm heading straight for it."

And now he's finally had to accept her invitation.

We all watch him carry her up the old road.

Tanya's stepmother is standing at the top of the steps, hip cocked, hand bracing her back. She shakes her poof-tied ponytail at Tanya as they pass, then plods along behind them to the car.

The neighbors are still standing around tut-tutting. You'd think they'd be embarrassed to admit they'd seen Tanya, Kirsten and Brandon on the log but hadn't done anything. Listen to them—making excuses to each other about why they didn't come down and try to shoo the kids off.

I guess Mom's had enough of being a sideshow. "Come on, kids. Let's go up to the cabin."

Fine with me. I'm pretty sick of explaining to all these people that no, the log did not hit me in the face.

"Kirsten, your eye!" Margo says as we start up. "Does it hurt?"

Kirsten's touches the spreading purple next to the

bridge of her nose. She nods. "I think Tanya's fist hit me when we fell."

"We'll put some ice on it."

I'm ready for Kirsten to start fretting about how horrible she's going to look, but she doesn't say a word.

Danny rolls the skimboard beside me. "Dad says you guys could've gotten killed." He and Jason have hurried back from up the beach to check out the commotion.

Brandon tugs at my sweatshirt sleeve and whispers in my ear. "Maybe this wouldn't have happened if I'd given Tanya a Returnity Belt. I didn't feel like it, though. I didn't like her."

"Neither did I," I whisper back. I don't feel too good about that now, but can you automatically start liking someone just because she got hurt? Maybe not. On the other hand, seeing Tanya like this . . . well, I sure couldn't hate her anymore—even if she came back with crutches and started acting bored and superior all over again. I guess I feel too sorry for her.

"Actually . . ." Brandon's face is all screwed up with big thoughts. "I don't think the Returnity Belt is what saved me."

"No?"

"No! You saved me!"

"Oh, come on," Jason says.

"Well, she did," Danny says. Then he gives Jason a sideways glance from under those long black eyelashes. "I'm glad somebody's sister has some sense."

Wow. I can't believe he said that. I want to let him

Linda Crew

know how much this means to me, but he won't meet my eyes.

"It's Uncle Jack!" Jason yells, spotting the Subaru that's pulled into the yard at Sea Haven.

I freeze. My face. Hey, I don't care if everyone north of Starr Street has seen it, Uncle Jack hasn't. Also, my clothes are a wreck. The rolled-up cuffs of my jeans are bagged down with wet sand.

I turn and bolt down the old road, back to the beach.

"Shelby!" Brandon yells. "Where you going?"

I just keep running across the sand, out to the rocks and my special place. Climbing in, I wrap my arms around my knees. All I hear is the pounding surf and my pounding heart. What am I going to do? No way can I face Uncle Jack like this. Uncle Jack and his fiancée.

I sit there until I lose track of time. I feel like sitting there forever.

They won't let me get away with that, though. After a while I see Uncle Jack down on the beach. I bet he's looking for me. This gets my heart thumping all over again. He's wearing a blue work shirt and jeans. The clouds have broken up now and the sun's come out to light up his golden hair. He's so handsome. I watch him walk over to the log that rolled. The tide's gone out now; the log's high and dry. He tries to shove it with his foot but it doesn't move. Then he starts walking toward the rocks—and me.

"Shelby? Shelby!"

I don't answer. I duck down. I can't decide if he's the last person I want to see or the first.

148

Someday I'll Laugh About This

He's whistling as he climbs up, heading straight for my special seat, leaping over the crevices where the waves try to crack open the rocks during winter storms.

"There you are," he says, coming over the high point and spotting me. "I figured I'd find you here."

He hooks his thumbs in his belt loops and takes in the view.

"Go away!" I bury my face between my knees.

"Hey, what kind of talk is that?"

Beats me. I mean, if I didn't want to see him, why would I hide here? Like he says, he knows how I feel about this place.

"I'm sorry," I say, "but I don't want you to see me."

"Aw, come on, Shelby. It's okay. Your mom explained what happened. Now let me see. I can take it."

I guess I can't put it off forever. Slowly I lift my face to him.

"Hmm. You *did* do a job on yourself, didn't you? And then Kirsten with that shiner." He shakes his head, amused. "Well, come on back to the cabin. We want to hear all about this log-rolling business. Nobody can figure out how you managed to lift it."

For just an instant I forget my face. "It *is* kind of weird," I say. "It's like I saw I had to move it, and for that second or two I got real strong."

He grins. "Tell you what, kiddo. You are something else."

Well, that Uncle Jack—he could coax a smile from a kid who's just discovered an empty Christmas stocking. I fight it, but darned if a little smile isn't stretching my scab tight.

He reaches a hand down to me. "Let's go meet Kate."

My smile collapses. "No, I just *can't*. Not like this."

"Well, what do you think you're going to do? Sit out here until your scab peels off? Because I'll tell you, the tide's going to come in and go out quite a few times before that happens."

"That's what I *feel* like doing."

"Shelby, if you don't come up, Kate's going to think you don't want to meet her."

"Oh." It hasn't even occurred to me that this Kate person might be worrying what I'd think of her.

"Besides, she's got fabric and patterns and I don't know what-all to show you. We want you and Kirsten to be bridesmaids, and she's going to sew your dresses herself."

"Yeah?" Suddenly I notice I'm shivering. Probably ought to get out of these damp, sandy clothes. "Well . . . okay." I let him help me up and I follow him across the rocks.

Back at the cabin, everyone's gathered on the front porch. As we climb the stone steps I try to scrunch my face down into my lowered sweatshirt hood. Then Mom steps aside and I see Uncle Jack's fiancée for the first time.

Cautiously I pull up out of my sweatshirt. I'm probably staring like a total space case as Jack leads me across the lawn. This is the girl he loves? The one he's decided is the best in the world?

Someday I'll Laugh About This

They're all watching me, waiting for my reaction. Well, here it is: I'm completely surprised, and somehow I'm not surprised at all. Looking at my new aunt-to-be, it's almost like something deep inside me is saying, "Of course."

Because this Kate is not the Kate I've been imagining. This Kate is actually kind of short, her hair is not some exotic shade, and if it wasn't for her braid, I'll bet it'd bush out all over.

What she does have is a wonderful, open face and a kind of a glow, a warmth I can almost feel.

This must be what Mrs. Blake means, I'm thinking. This must be heart.

But there's something more, something oddly familiar about her.

"Shelby," she says, "I've heard a lot about you."

"Yeah?"

"I told her you two were a lot alike," Uncle Jack says. "I never could resist a smart-mouthed woman."

"Oh, you!" Kate elbows him.

"Well, they keep you on your toes." He winks at me.

Kate's looking at my face. Not, oh-how-gross, just kind of matter-of-fact and sympathetic.

"I don't usually look like this," I manage.

Everybody laughs.

"Sure does take me back," Kate says. "I did something like that to myself once—burned my face with a sunlamp trying to get a quick tan. I was the only dancing beet at our senior prom."

"You never told me that story," Jack says.

"Didn't I? Well, I probably have enough dumb-things-I've-done stories to last us the rest of our lives." She shakes her head. "I'll tell you one thing, though—I never thought I'd be able to laugh about that like I do now!"

Right then I know I'm going to love having Kate in our family.

Epilogue

Before we left Sea Haven, I wrote about Tanya in the logbook. Not all the details, of course, and in the great tradition of Gramma B., hardly any of the feelings. How could I ever put those down so anyone else could understand? I couldn't understand a lot of the feelings myself, and I'm the one who felt them!

But I made sure I put in enough juicy hints so that maybe someday, some evening when we're sitting around the fire having hot chocolate and talking about old times, our kids will read the logbook and go, "Tanya Dymond? Who the heck was Tanya Dymond?"

Then Kirsten and I can argue about it in front of them —each tell our own version of what really happened. Maybe in twenty years it'll be a safer subject.

In the meantime the log rolling had shocked us into a sort of truce. At least we were on speaking terms again.

Both of us were surprised when Tanya got grounded for her part in the accident. It seemed kind of unfair. Even though her leg wasn't actually broken, she got banged up pretty bad. Wasn't that punishment enough?

But the biggest surprise wasn't Tanya's grounding—it was her reaction to it. I thought she'd have a fit—run away or something. But she loved it! Suddenly, getting grounded was the greatest thing since MTV.

"They watch me all the time," she told us when we went up to visit her on her patio. "I'm like this prisoner."

So are you bragging or complaining? I thought. But I kept my mouth shut. I think I knew, anyway. Every time she'd glance over her shoulder and catch her dad at the window, she'd roll her eyes, but the smile tugging at the corner of her mouth was definitely smug.

Jack and Kate only stayed for two days, and whenever I think of that second week at Sea Haven, I think of sitting around Tanya's patio talking about them.

"I just don't get it," Kirsten must have said a hundred times. "I always thought Uncle Jack would marry somebody who . . . well, a . . ."

"A magazine model?" I finally said.

"Well, no, not really, but—"

"But someone who *looks* like one?"

She sighed. "I guess so."

Instead he'd decided to marry a real person. How about that?

"Come on," Tanya said. "Your uncle Jack isn't *that* much of a fox. You guys just think so because you like him."

I didn't have a snappy answer at the time, but later I thought, Yeah, that's right, and so what? Because wasn't it like what Mom said? How you feel about people doesn't always depend on how they look. It's more the other way around—how they look to you depends on how you feel.

Kirsten and I never did hash all this out—who was

right, who was wrong, who'd been acting immature. And maybe that's for the best. Her magazines are full of junk about communication and getting to the bottom of things with other people, but sometimes I think it's smarter just to put bad stuff behind you and move on.

By the end of the vacation we had pretty much quit sniping at each other, and by the time Uncle Jack's wedding rolled around in late September, I had to admit I was actually looking forward to seeing Kirsten again.

The Friday afternoon they were supposed to arrive, Mom had me out washing the salty gunk off the windows. I could see her working inside, taking a broom to the rafters. Sea Haven had to be all spiffed up for Jack and Kate's honeymoon.

I squirted each pane with cleaner and wiped until my face came clear in the glass. I wasn't afraid to look, now that my clown smile was history. I'll say this for my crash beauty treatment, it did work in one way. Kind of like the old oatmeal facial—so grody, you *had* to look better when it was over! Thank goodness the last traces of my botched effort peeled away over Labor Day weekend. I'd have died if I'd had to start school that way.

School. I kept on squirting the windows. Wonder how it was going for Kirsten this year. And where the heck were they, anyway?

Every time I got down to move the ladder I'd go take a peek up the road to see if their car was coming. Then I'd look up the beach—almost high tide by now, and the white waves rolling in one after another, just the way they do day after day, year after year. It may sound strange, but it always sort of gets to me to remember that they do this all the time, whether we're here or not. . . .

September at the Oregon coast is a really special time. The air is warm and still, nicer than the usual summer days when the inland heat makes it foggy here. So fall is the best time, but hardly anybody gets in on it. We can never be here that long, so every hour is precious as gold. The only catch about late September is dark coming earlier.

I finished the windows. The grass under my bare feet was getting cold as I picked up the wads of used paper towels. Just when the sun dipped south of the house on the point, the cousins' mini-van finally pulled in.

"Hey, your scab's gone." That's the first thing Kirsten said to me when she jumped out onto the lawn. "Wow, I'll bet that's a relief."

I nodded. "And no scar."

Forgetting to play it cool, we smiled at each other.

Then she turned and checked for lights at the house on the point.

"Nobody there," I said.

She shrugged.

That was the closest we came to mentioning Tanya the weekend of the wedding.

Our moms kept us busy all day Saturday getting ready for the reception—truly a do-it-yourself affair. You couldn't buy potato salad like Mom's anywhere, which meant a lot of peeling for Kirsten and me. The boys had to help by hauling up driftwood that Dad and Uncle Don split and stacked in the garage. A honeymoon was a big deal. You were supposed to laze around—not work.

On Sunday morning we had to pack as much as possible before the wedding. The plan was for us to clean up from the party and clear out while Jack and Kate ate dinner at a restaurant, just the two of them.

Mom stripped the best double bed and then handed me a stack of brand-new sheets, still in their plastic wrappings.

"Get Kirsten to help you put these on, and do a real nice job, okay?" She handed me a card in an envelope. "Tuck this in so Jack and Kate'll know the sheets are a gift."

Well, it was funny. Kirsten and I had no sooner gotten that first bottom sheet stretched across the mattress than I looked at her and started to giggle.

Her face got red, thinking the same thing I was thinking—about what was going to happen on these very sheets tonight.

"Come on, Shelby," she pleaded.

"I can't help it!"

Then she cracked up, too, and that was it—five seconds later we were helplessly out of control. My stomach muscles ached and the flowers on the sheets blurred in front of me.

"Well!" Mom said, appearing at the door, watching us doubled over. "If I'd known how much you two enjoy sheet changing, I'd have asked you to do it more often." Then she called into the living room. "Hey Margo, come check this out."

Linda Crew

Margo peeked around the doorjamb. We were still giggling like crazy. Kirsten's red face streamed tears.

"Honeymoon humor," Mom explained.

Margo smirked, folding her arms over her chest. "Looks like they take after us, huh?"

" 'Fraid so," Mom said.

"Well, they could do worse, right?"

"Right!"

Now I've noticed that when you really look forward to something, it's often a letdown. But the things you dread usually don't turn out as bad as you think. Not that you can spend your life in constant dread as insurance against disappointment—that would be totally hazardous to your health!

But I had never been able to help hating the idea of Uncle Jack getting married. Maybe that's why when it finally happened, it wasn't so bad. I guess all I'd ever thought of was losing him. I never thought of gaining somebody like Kate, who is genuinely terrific, as even Kirsten now agrees.

We had the wedding up on top of Cape Perpetua in the little stone lookout—almost like a chapel. It was clear and warm, the best day possible. They had a man with a guitar and another with one of those little wooden flutey things playing the kind of music you hear on PBS. When they started a certain tune, Kirsten and I and Kate's older sister, Becca, carried flowers down from the woods into the little building, our long dresses trailing on the path.

Mine was pale blue and floaty, and when I first put it

158

on, I didn't feel like me at all. I felt like somebody at least sixteen, and I had to think hard about every step I took. But pretty soon it felt okay—after all, this was me, too, wasn't it? Like Dad had pointed out, I wasn't always going to be twelve. This could be sort of a practice run at being my older self.

So by the time I walked down the path, I was getting used to the idea that I looked nice. Then I saw Mom and Dad watching me, and rats . . . my face felt like I'd fried it all over again, I got so flustered. My own parents, but somehow I felt shy at all this . . . well . . . *love* they were beaming out at me.

We turned and watched Kate coming in her crown of baby's breath. Her dress was simple, almost medieval-looking, with a flower-laced cord looped low around her hips. The warm breeze fluttered the filmy sleeves. Suddenly I flashed on a picture from an old storybook of mine. I wouldn't have been surprised if a fawn had nuzzled up next to her or a bird had fluttered to her shoulder.

She and Jack stood with the minister in front of the stone arches that framed the ocean's horizon. First the minister talked about marriage and how it was a sacrament and something about all of us being in a state of grace. Grace meant love unearned, he said. He went on about Jack and Kate hanging in there together through the hard times and all, but I was still thinking about love unearned. I liked that. It just about summed this whole family business up, didn't it? Love even when you don't deserve it, love in spite of everybody's awkward stages.

159

Then Jack and Kate said their vows—a mixture of churchy stuff and words they thought up themselves. Far above the ocean as we were, the thunder of the breakers below couldn't reach us. The only sounds were Kate and Jack whispering, and the rustle of the fresh wind in the firs.

That and the sound of everybody sniffing like crazy.

I cried, too—not just your standard wedding mushiness, either. A lot of it was relief that I felt okay about Uncle Jack getting married. And since he had chosen Kate, it no longer seemed like the impossible dream that someday somebody would look at me the way he was looking at her now.

Besides, it was good being reminded that life does have high points like this, wonderful times when for a little while at least, everybody is trying real hard, all at the same time, to "make things nice."

The following summer, under court order, the county workers took down and hauled away Max Dymond's chain-link fencing.

The very next day, Kirsten and I walked to the Perpetua Post Office, just like we had so many times before. Neither of us got any letters, but neither of us cared much, either. Kirsten was between death-to-be-apart boyfriends and even surprised me by spending her money on a couple of paperbacks instead of makeup.

Heading back to the cabin, I felt great. The sky was blue, the wind carried a good beachy smell of wood smoke, and we had two weeks at Sea Haven ahead of us.

Someday I'll Laugh About This

Gramma and Grampa B. had come that morning; Jack and Kate would be arriving any time. It'd be Sleeping Bag City—for the weekend, anyway.

Everyone had to be here for the party celebrating the winning of the court case against Max Dymond's fences. All the neighbors were going to walk the road together, and Mrs. Blake said the TV news people from Eugene were even going to come.

Good old Mrs. Blake. Just like she'd promised, she showed us how tough it can be to fight an old hothead—especially an old hothead smart enough to act like a sweet little old lady when she testifies at hearings.

The Dymonds' beach house now had two big red FOR SALE signs on it.

Looking at them, Kirsten stopped. Then she turned to me. "Did I tell you Tanya wrote me?"

"No, really? What'd she say?"

"Well, she broke up with Shawn, but she didn't sound too bent out of shape about it." She started walking again. "Says her little brother is pretty cute, after all. Actually, she sounded a lot happier than last summer."

"Hmm." I was a lot happier, too. After all, everyone said that the journal entries that I'd read at the hearings helped a lot. But somehow there was more to my mood than winning the road fight. I tossed my hair back in the breeze, enjoying the fling of my new beaded hair ribbons —not the ones Kirsten liked best, the ones I chose. I knew they looked good, and if Jason tried to tease me, I'd just freeze him out. He'd learn fast what Danny found

Linda Crew

out months ago—namely that my shove-and-wrestle days were gone for good.

I turned and walked backward in front of Kirsten on the trail. "Do you think maybe we just happened to meet Tanya when she was having the most bummed-out summer of her life?"

"Maybe." Kirsten made a face. "I sure wouldn't want anybody judging *me* by the way I acted last year."

"Me, neither," I said, spinning to face forward again. Was Kirsten trying to apologize? "Maybe all three of us should have been packed off to Camp Awkward Stage."

"Come again?"

"Oh, never mind." I smiled, shoving my hands into my windbreaker pockets. "You know, you really ought to keep writing to her."

"But Shelby, you hated her."

"Not really. Well, maybe I thought I did." Funny how time has a way of watering down some of the bad parts. Already I was thinking of Tanya with a certain affection. "She kept things interesting, anyway." I stopped and looked at the house on the point for a moment.

Kirsten caught up and stood beside me. "Maybe *you* ought to write to her."

"You kidding? She was *your* friend. Besides, what could I say? 'Please write me the continuing story of your life because you're so interesting and unpredictable'?"

Kirsten laughed. "Anyway, it's hard to stay friends with somebody just by letters, isn't it?"

"Yeah." The time between letters from Jane had been stretching out longer and longer. I'd written her about

162

Someday I'll Laugh About This

this boy I kind of like, but he's new in Corvallis and Jane's never met him, so it probably wasn't too interesting to her, just like I have a hard time putting faces on the people she writes about to me. It doesn't mean I don't like her anymore. It's just the way it is.

It's different with relatives, though. Even when you're apart, you're more likely to keep up with what's going on —especially if your mothers yak on the phone a lot. Besides, you go way back with cousins—all those things you remember together. Makes it easier to pick up where you left off, even if remembering does mean remembering which things you can't talk about.

So we kicked along the sandy trail, not saying anything for a while. After all our tense silences, it was nice to get back to the comfortable kind. We scrambled down into one of the dips where the winter tides had eroded the bank. I knew every step of this trail by heart, and it sure did feel good to be walking it again.

"Hey, look at that," Kirsten said as we climbed up out of the gully. From behind the salal bushes, a huge bubble was rising over Sea Haven.

"Wow!" I stepped up my pace, eyes on the bubble. Here came two more, floating upward. These were no puny bubbles, the kind you make out of little plastic bottles that get passed out as birthday-party favors. These were a foot or two across. As we got closer I could see them shimmering, purple and blue and gold.

I turned to Kirsten and grinned. "Somehow I get the feeling Uncle Jack and Kate are here."

We ducked under the arching shore pine and found

everyone gathered in the front yard, dipping these red plastic wands with ropy things on the ends into lemony-smelling buckets of soapy water. Even Mrs. Blake was there, watching a large bubble form in the loop of her wand. Her eyes looked bright, like a kid's. The bubble broke free and floated up. Everyone cheered, then laughed as it collapsed and fell as a quick liquid sparkle.

Kate spotted us. "Shelby! Kirsten!"

"Aren't these great?" Brandon said. "Uncle Jack brought them."

"Oh really? Gee, I never would have guessed."

"Here," Uncle Jack said, taking a wand from Jason. "Let an expert show you how this is done."

I watched him dip the wand in the bucket and pull it out. His face reminded me of Brandon's—this look of total concentration, as if the bubble he was about to make was the most important thing in the world. And watching him, here's what I was thinking: Some good things do last. Uncle Jack was married, and sure, that was bound to change him some. But deep down he was still the same old Uncle Jack I loved. And he always would be.

He held up the wand and slowly, slowly eased out the biggest, most amazing bubble. Honestly, that thing was at least three feet across.

Of course, when we talked about this later, Daddy insisted on explaining about color spectrums and air currents and optical illusions, but as for me, well . . . I know magic when I see it.

"Aaaaaahh!" everyone breathed as Uncle Jack's bubble hovered above us. No one said a word. No one wanted to break the spell.

This incredible golden bubble just hung there, wobbling above us. We were all in it. I could see our wondering, upturned faces reflecting back at us. And as it rose, I could even see the cabin. Sea Haven. We squinted as it went right up into the sun.

We all watched that bubble for the longest time, but we never did see it burst.

I like to think it kept right on going.

How do four girls meet four boys?
They advertise for pen pals, of course!

Sharon Dennis Wyeth